# PLAYING THE CARDS YOU'RE DEALT

**ALSO BY VARIAN JOHNSON**

*Twins*

*The Parker Inheritance*

*To Catch a Cheat*

*The Great Greene Heist*

# PLAYING THE CARDS YOU'RE DEALT

VARIAN JOHNSON

Scholastic Press
*New York*

Library of Congress Cataloging-in-Publication Data available
ISBN 978-1-338-34853-8

1 2021

Printed in the U.S.A. 23

First edition, October 2021

Book design by Abby Dening

FOR DAD

# CHAPTER 1

*The house always wins.*

At least, that's what us card sharks say when things don't go our way. It's an old saying about gamblers. No matter how skilled, sharp, or slick you *think* you are—if you ain't smart enough to quit when you're ahead, you'll eventually lose all of your hard-earned money to the "house." Which, for all you youngbloods out there who don't know better, means the casino.

The house. It is all powerful. It sets the rules, it stacks the odds in its favor, and given enough time, it's unbeatable.

Now, every Joplin man worth his salt knows this—even young Anthony. But the thing is, the saying doesn't just apply to casinos. You see, when it comes to *family* matters, what Ant's daddy usually says is: *Your* mother *is the house, and the house always wins.*

And that was for sure the truth this morning. Before Ant even touched the knob to the back door, his mom appeared in the kitchen with hands on hips, lips pursed, and eyeballs zeroed in on him.

As us OGs used to say back in the day, youngblood was cold busted.

"Where do you think you're going?" his mother asked. She was already dressed in her usual getup of navy-blue scrubs and white sneakers.

"To school?" Ant offered.

"This early? Without letting me or your father know?"

"I left a note." He offered a sly smile. "I thought you'd be happy that I was trying to be early on the first day."

"Umm-hmm," his mother said, eyeing the torn half sheet of paper Ant had left on the kitchen table. The boy had even tacked on *Love, Anthony* at the end of the note—a little sugar to soothe the sting of slipping out on his parents.

Let's be honest—everybody in that kitchen knew that Ant wasn't getting up all early because he was excited for school. It was more that he didn't want his parents to *walk* him to school on the first day. He knew his mom was already gearing up to take a gazillion photos of him—first at home, then out on the front porch, and then again next to the big sign by the front doors of Gerald Elementary. Meanwhile, his daddy was probably prepping for one of his legendary first-day-walk-to-school pep talks. Last year's talk was about peer pressure, and the year before was about focusing in class. Ant had a sneaking suspicion that his father was going to spring The Talk on him this year—the one too embarrassing to name—and there was no way he was sticking around to hear that. Ant wasn't even interested in holding hands or swapping spit in the first place. Plus, the way he saw it, most of the girls he knew were too bossy, anyway.

So no, Ant didn't want any part of his daddy's talk this morning.

And coincidentally . . . if he left early, he figured that his momma wouldn't be able to ask him about the deck of playing cards stashed at the bottom of his backpack.

His mother finally finished reading the note. "Nice try, sweetie. You get an A for effort. But I didn't move my shift around this morning just for you to sneak off on me. Now sit down. I'll scramble some eggs."

Ant scrunched up his nose. "Does it *have* to be eggs?"

"Keep talking, and I'll make grits instead."

Ant clamped his mouth shut. He wasn't a big fan of grits—he thought they tasted like bland, soupy white rice. When his grandma cooked them, he could usually dump enough salt or cheese on them to make 'em edible. But Yolanda Joplin—bless her heart—wasn't exactly skilled in the cooking department. His momma's grits came out more like hard grains of white sand. Wasn't enough salt or cheese in the world to save them.

Ant trudged back to the table and shrugged off his backpack. He didn't get why everyone was working themselves into a tizzy about the first day of school. It wasn't like anything was changing. It was the same building and same students. Honestly, he was looking right forward to returning to something familiar, especially given how much some things had changed at home.

Or rather, how much *someone* had changed.

# CHAPTER 2

Ten minutes later, Yolanda Joplin beamed as she plopped a plate down in front of her baby boy. Unfortunately, Ant didn't see anything to smile about. His momma had cooked "Cajun" style again.

In other words, she'd burned the eggs. And the sausage. And even the toast.

Ant picked up his fork, mentally preparing himself for a mouthful of char, but before he could even take a bite, his parents' bedroom door creaked open. Ant looked at his mother.

"Don't worry," she said as she returned to the stove. "He's in a really good mood this morning."

Sure enough, Ant's father came striding down the hallway, wearing that classic Joplin grin. He even had on a fancy sports coat—you know, the type with the patches on the elbows—and loafers so shiny that they looked like glass. "Ant! Ready for the first day of school?"

Ant smiled—just as much because of his father's good mood as his clothes. "Whoa! You look gooood, Dad!"

"Surprised your pops can still clean up?" Roland Joplin tugged at his collar, making his tie crooked. "Though maybe I need to invest in a few new shirts. Your mom must have shrunk these by accident."

"Yeah, or somebody's midsection expanded," Ant's mother said as she prepared another plate.

"What can I say? I don't want to look *too* perfect. Don't want to make y'all jealous." His father sat down. "But forget about me, Ant. Let's talk about *you*."

Ant shook his head like a windshield wiper on full speed. "No, tell me why you're dressed up," he said. "It's because of your meeting with Mr. Monroe, right? Are you ready for it?"

"It's with one of his kids, actually. But let me worry about that." His father propped his elbow on the table. "So here you are, about to start fifth grade. The king of spades in a pack of clubs. A big joker in a deck of deuces. A jack of—"

"Roland, don't encourage him."

"Sorry. Just trying to get on my man's level. Old card shark to young card shark." He winked. "Anyway, now that you're a year older, you might find that you're having strange feelings in all parts of your body—"

"Ma! Need help with Dad's eggs?"

His mother laughed as she walked over and set a plate down in front of her husband. "Really, Roland? You want to have this conversation now?"

"Just trying to prep him. You know, I was only a few years older than Ant is when I met you . . ."

"Then why did it take you so long to ask me out?"

"Oh, you know me." He grinned like a kid on Christmas morning. "I was too busy dating Joyce. And then there was Iesha. And then Kadija from around the way . . ." He put his hands over his heart. "You were too much of a good girl for me."

Ant glanced at his mom. She was thinking up the perfect comeback. He could see it on her face.

"The way I remember it," she finally said, "you and your high-water pants weren't dating anybody."

"Ohh!" Ant said, cackling at his father. "She said *high waters*."

"Didn't you go to your senior prom with your cousin?" his mom continued.

Ant elbowed his father. "She said you ain't got no game, Dad."

"The new school year's starting up, Ant," his mother said. "How about you replace *ain't* with something more grammatically correct?"

"Technically, it isn't wrong, it's just slang. Aaron says that Black slang should be just as acceptable as regular English." Ant's sixteen-year-old brother, Aaron, had lots of opinions on the matter. "He says it's only cultural bias that—"

"Cultural bias ain't going to get you into Mitchell Academy," Ant's father said.

Ant frowned. "But you just used *ain't*?"

"As my daddy used to tell me, 'Do as I say, not as I do.'" Roland turned to Yolanda. "And speaking of technicalities—my prom date was only a cousin by marriage, which we all know doesn't really count. And I liked those high pants. They were functional. They kept my ankles cool."

"Whatever the case, you're lucky I took pity on you." Ant's mother draped her arm around her husband and gave him a big wet kiss, right on the lips. "Against my better judgment."

The sight of Yolanda's mahogany-brown cheeks against Roland's pecan-tan skin would have made most people swoon, but it just made Ant gag.

"Can't you guys wait until I leave?" he asked, trying his best to scrub that smooching sound from his memory. "You know, like, for college?"

"Don't worry," his father replied. "You'll be leaving soon enough. Keep those grades up, and before you know it, you'll be at Mitchell for high school like your brother."

"We have plenty of time to focus on Mitchell Academy." She pointed to Ant's plate. "Right now, you need to eat so I can snap some photos before school."

"Ma . . ."

"Just do it," his father added, picking up his toast. "You've lost this hand before it's even been dealt. The house always—"

"Roland." She sighed. "Enough with the card references."

If you haven't figured out by now, Ant's father was big-time into card games. He could play almost any game, but his favorites were tonk and spades and bid whist. Games that he'd learned to play from *his* pop. Games that he taught to his own two kids—Ant and Aaron.

In fact, it was a Joplin man tradition to play in the

Oak Grove spades tournament . . . and win. Aaron had already proven his worth, winning the teen tournament twice in a row. Ant had competed last year as well, in the junior division. But unlike Aaron's, Ant's results were . . . well, let's just say they were less than satisfactory.

Ant had felt so bad, he hadn't even stuck around to see his brother win. And the oversized grin on his daddy's face when Aaron came waltzing into the house carrying that big old trophy was enough to break Ant's little heart. His father hadn't looked at Ant like that once during his games.

But a year had passed. Ant was older, smarter, and just plain better. And now it was time for him to make up for past shortcomings. Plus, since his brother wouldn't be home from boarding school to compete in this year's tournament, it was all on Ant to uphold the family legacy. To raise that trophy over *his* head while everyone clapped and cheered.

*That's* why he wanted to get to school early. The tournament was in two weeks—the Saturday before Labor Day—and he needed to get in as much practice as he could.

Ant scarfed down his breakfast—char and all—then jumped up from the table. "Done!" He smiled at his mother. “Ma, I’m not sure if we have time for all those pictures this morning.”

“Still angling to get out of us walking with you, huh,” she said. “Or are you just trying to leave before I ask you about that deck of cards in your backpack?”

Now, for a ten-year-old, young Anthony was a skilled bluffer. Cool as the fur on a polar bear’s bottom. Ant could have lied about those cards tucked away in his backpack without breaking a sweat.

But there was another old saying that Roland had taught both of his kids—wisdom passed down from his own pop. In the immortal words of the patron saint of card players, Kenny Rogers, also known as The Gambler: *You’ve got to know when to hold them, know when to fold them*.

Ant fished the deck of cards out of his bag and handed them to his father. They weren’t just any cards, but Unicycles—the *only* cards that a true spades player used. The deck was old, but the cards were still crisp enough to make a solid *thwap* when slapped on the table.

Ant watched his father cut the cards with one hand. Ant had been practicing, but his fingers weren’t long enough for that yet. The size of his hands, like the rest of his body, seemed to be lagging behind everyone else in his grade.

"I was thinking about asking Jamal to come over after school so we can get some more practice in," Ant said. "Is that okay?"

"*Okay*? That's *exactly* what you should be doing!" His father made another one-handed cut. "We'll play when I get home. Me and your momma against you two knuckleheads. If my meeting goes well, I should be home by four at the latest." He leaned close to Ant and whispered, "This year, you're gonna *slaughter* the competition. I know it. Just gotta toughen you up a little more."

Even though Ant kept right on grinning, his insides curled into a tight ball. "Thanks, Dad."

"You know, you could just play for fun," Ant's mother said lightly as she walked over and took the cards from her husband. "*Both* of y'all can have these back this afternoon." She checked the clock. "Alright, let's get a move on. Gwendolyn is only covering me for a few hours."

Roland's megawatt smile faded. "Oh. That's why you're still here. I thought that maybe you decided to go back to working your regular shift. They must be paying you a lot more money to be such an early riser . . ."

"You know me. I like being up before everyone else."

Then she kept right on talking, like a fire hose with a broken nozzle, trying her best to blast past Roland's sour look. "Okay, Anthony, or should I say—Mr. Big-Time Fifth Grader. I suppose you're old enough to walk to school by yourself on the first day . . . as soon as I get some pictures."

Ant groaned.

"Just a few, sweetie. I promise. Now where did I put that phone . . ."

Ant looked at his father. "A little help here?"

Roland was still frowning. Still sour.

"Dad?"

Roland blinked. "Huh, what was that?"

"Can you tell Ma I'm too old for pictures?"

Roland chuckled, and just like that, the moodiness was gone. "You want some advice, Ant?" He cleared his throat . . . then started to sing. *"You got to know when to hold 'em—"*

Ant covered his ears. "Dad!"

*"Know when to fold 'em—"*

"You're supposed to be on my side!" Ant pleaded.

His father stopped singing long enough to shoot Ant an amused grin. Then he turned toward his wife. "Your phone's in the bedroom, honey. I'll grab it." He rose from

. "And, Ant, don't you know—a spades player

acks up his partner."

nother old saying.

His father headed down the hallway, swaying back and forth, singing all the way to his room. *"Know when to walk away . . . Know when to run . . ."*

# CHAPTER 3

After forty-six photos and way too many kisses to count, Ant finally headed to school. His parents stayed by the door, watching and waving while he skedaddled down the porch steps. The temperature was cool for late August—a last-minute summer storm was due to be coming through. His mother had forced him to stuff a jacket, hat, and umbrella in his backpack—just in case. She had even tried to get him to wear one of those clear plastic ponchos, but thankfully his father stepped in and vetoed that idea. No kid wanted to look like a walking Hefty bag on the first day of school.

Still, Ant was shivering by the time he reached the end of the street. He was afraid that his mother was going to march after him and make him put on that jacket after all.

But it turned out that he didn't have to worry about that, 'cause when he looked back for one last wave to his parents, he realized that they'd already gone inside the house.

*Good,* Ant told himself. He was glad that his parents weren't still there, staring at him as he walked away. He was glad that they realized he was big enough to do this by himself.

Or at least, he was *mostly* glad.

It did feel a little strange, if he was being right honest with himself. His parents had always tagged along on the first day of school, their shadows blending together as they walked down the sidewalk. And while he didn't want to hear his dad's pep talk or spend the rest of the day rubbing his mom's lipstick smudges from his cheek, when he saw his classmates posing by the flagpole and hugging their parents goodbye, he felt a smidgen of regret.

He pulled out his phone and started to text Aaron, but before he could even finish the message, a note from his brother popped onto the screen.

**Have a good first day of school!**

**Don't get into any trouble!**

That was Aaron Joplin for you . . . always two steps ahead. Ant's brother was smart, confident, a great musician, and an excellent student. If he hadn't also been such a nice guy and a good brother, Ant would've hated him.

Ant quickly typed in his response: **Just left the house. Was able to talk Ma and Dad into letting me walk by myself**.

A few seconds later, Aaron's replied: **What?! Little man is growing up!**

Ant's jaw tightened like a wrench around a pipe. He closed the message, then stuffed his phone way down deep into his pocket. He knew he was supposed to come back at his brother with something funny—kinda like how his momma and daddy had been going back and forth at each other during breakfast—but Aaron's text struck a little too close to home.

When Ant was younger, he'd liked his nickname. After all, ants were kinda cool as far as insects went. Super strong for their size. Only now that everyone at school—even the girls—had shot up past him in height, it didn't feel so good anymore. And no one, including his brother, seemed to want him to forget that.

But even with all the teasing, Ant still missed his brother.

Just a few days earlier, Aaron had left to start his junior

year at Mitchell Academy, a private boarding school in the Blue Ridge Mountains, about four hours away. It had always been their father's dream for the boys to attend the pretentious—I mean, *prestigious*—school, and Aaron, with his good grades and high SAT scores, had finally been accepted last year. If his daddy had anything to say about it, Ant would be there soon enough, too.

He knew that he was supposed to be happy for Aaron, but he wasn't. Things had been weird around the house ever since his brother—or really, their *father*—had decided that Aaron was going to that school. Ant knew his mom was worried about paying for it. It was no secret that Mitchell was expensive. Or that Roland Joplin's accounting business wasn't doing so well. But Ant's dad had insisted that a man was only as smart as the teachers he had or as lucky as the friends he made. Going to a respected school like Mitchell would introduce Aaron to all sorts of movers and shakers and give him every opportunity to succeed in life. He said the bills were worth it, but Ant wasn't so sure.

The week before his brother left, their father had been in a particularly long funk about a client who'd dumped him for a larger accounting firm.

Ant had been worried, but Aaron told him not to

sweat it. "As bad as things seem now, it's nothing like they were BEFORE," Aaron said. "And if we can make it through that, we can make it through anything."

BEFORE happened nine years ago, when Ant was just a baby.

BEFORE was a stretch of time when their dad didn't live with them.

BEFORE was when their father was in rehab.

"Make it through what, exactly?" he'd asked Aaron. He'd tried to get the lowdown a million times. But his brother always just said *I'll tell you when you're older.* Ant may have been old enough to walk to school by himself on the first day of fifth grade, but apparently he wasn't old enough to know the full story.

But Ant wasn't no dummy. He'd overheard enough conversations to know that rehab had something to do with drinking. His father must have gone to stay at one of those fancy six-week treatment centers that all the famous celebrities went to when they'd been caught drinking and driving and stuff like that.

Ant wished he could talk to his best friend, Jamal, about BEFORE. But a real Joplin man didn't air his dirty laundry.

Or his family's.

# CHAPTER 4

Speaking of Jamal, he and Ant were supposed to meet right by the school sign that morning. Even with the delay at home, Ant was on time. Jamal, on the other hand, was the type of fella who'd be late to his own funeral.

After a few minutes of waiting around, Ant walked back to the playground. Then he tried the front steps. And then the carpool lane. He was about to pull out his phone when he finally caught sight of Jamal making his way across the intersection, strutting like a peacock on a hot summer day.

"Wassup, Ant!" Jamal said once he reached the other side of the crosswalk. "Sorry I'm late."

"No problem. It's cool," Ant said, even though it wasn't. Jamal had spent most of July and August in Philadelphia, visiting his dad, and Ant wasn't sure, but his friend looked like he'd grown at least a half an inch.

Ain't it a shame when the tall get even taller?

"Ma caught me before I left home and made me turn over my deck." Ant arched an eyebrow. "Any chance you were able to get your hands on some cards?"

Ant was smart enough to suspect his mother would confiscate his pack, so he'd come up with a backup plan. You see, Aaron wasn't the only Joplin capable of thinking two steps ahead.

Jamal riffled through his backpack. "Yeah, I got them, but . . ." He pulled out a pack of cards held together by a thick rubber band. "I don't know if it's a full deck."

Ant picked up the pack with his index finger and thumb and held it up like it was a mangy dead possum he didn't want to get too close to. The cards were old and creased. The ace of hearts was on top and covered with grease stains. At least, he hoped they were grease stains. Jamal had two little cousins at home. They were always drooling over everything.

Drooling. And peeing.

"Please tell me you didn't find these in Bailey and Donovan's room," Ant said.

"No, fool. I got them out the packet drawer. That's just

soy sauce on there. I think." Jamal reached for the cards. "Look, we don't have to use them if you don't—"

"Just wait up, alright?" Ant said, pulling the deck back. He undid the rubber band and quickly counted the cards. Fifty-four. All present and accounted for, even the jokers. He pulled the deuces of hearts and diamonds out of the deck, then refastened the rubber band around the remaining cards. "Think we'd have time to get a game in before the bell—"

*RING!!!*

Well, that answered that.

"Come on," Ant said, starting toward the door. "Maybe we can play during lunch."

"Hold up a second," Jamal said. "What's the point of rushing to class? The quicker we get there, the quicker we'll have to get to work."

"You're just hoping to see Erika, aren't you?"

"Naw," Jamal said, though his smile signaled otherwise. "But—and I'm just curious now—how do I look?"

Ant laughed as he looked Jamal up and down. His friend had been pining after Erika del Rosario for the past year—ever since she'd said that she liked a shirt he was wearing. A shirt so hideous, it would give the boogeyman nightmares. Either Erika was being really nice, or she was one of the only people on the planet who liked the color of fresh vomit. Still, Jamal held on to that comment like a starving man trying to get the last scrap of meat off of a bone and wore the shirt every chance he got.

Of course, Jamal had yet to actually have a real conversation with Erika, but maybe that would change this year.

As the boys watched everyone *except* Erika del Rosario enter the school, Ant noticed how different the kids looked this year. Older. Bigger. Taller.

He wondered if anyone would say the same about him.

"Maybe she'll be in our class," Jamal mused once they joined the stragglers. "Or maybe I'll see her at—" He paused as he took in a sharp breath. *"Booker at ten o'clock!"* Jamal hissed.

"What are you, a spy?" Ant asked.

"Just wanted to make sure you could see her." He nudged him. "You know, given how tall the crowd is."

"Low blow, Jamal," Ant muttered as he stuffed the deck into his pocket. It wasn't that playing cards were banned at school . . . but then again, why take chances?

"Good morning, Mr. Joplin. Mr. Williams," Mrs. Booker said. "Excited about the new year?"

"Yes, ma'am," they both mumbled.

When they were out of earshot, Jamal asked, "Is it

weird that your aunt calls you by your last name at school?"

"She's not my real aunt," Ant said. "But yeah, you have a point."

Even though Mrs. Booker had been the assistant principal at Gerald Elementary School for three years, Ant had known her for a lot longer. Not only had she grown up in the Oak Grove neighborhood, like his parents, but she and his mom had gone to college together. When Ant first saw pictures of Mrs. Booker and his momma from Florida A&M University, with their matching pink-and-green jackets, crop-top T-shirts, and way-way-way-too-skinny jeans, he couldn't quite process it. He couldn't imagine his mom—or really, any adult—ever being young. He'd always thought that all grown-ups came into the world with sore backs, wire-rimmed glasses, and the need for "fiscal responsibility." But knowing that Mrs. Booker was more than just an assistant principal only made it weirder whenever he saw her.

Eventually, the boys made it to the fifth-grade hall. Mr. Reese, their new teacher, stood by the classroom door. He'd been at the school for a lot longer than Mrs. Booker, though you wouldn't have known it by how he looked.

If Ant had seen this fella somewhere else, like at the

mall or the park, he would have guessed that Mr. Reese was in high school. Maybe college. With that scraggly blond soul patch under his bottom lip, the untucked (and wrinkled) polo shirt, and baby-blue high-tops, Mr. Reese looked like one of those white guys who was trying too hard to be cool in front of the *homeboys*.

Though Ant had to admit, Mr. Reese's shoes were *nice*.

"Welcome to class, Jamal and Anthony!" he said, before giving each of the boys an overenthusiastic high five. "Come on in and take your seat. We're going to spend the first few minutes of class writing a letter about what you did during the summer. You can go ahead and get started."

The boys entered their classroom and immediately froze.

"I thought you said we were sitting together," Jamal said.

"I thought we *were*."

When he and his mom had dropped off his materials last week, Ant had been sure to pick the desk beside Jamal's—in a cluster of desks with three other boys. But now Holly was sitting in his seat.

Ant turned back toward the door, but Mr. Reese was already stepping inside the room.

"Oh snap," Mr. Reese said. And then he *actually*

snapped. "I forgot—I had to mix things up. Couldn't have all the boys sitting separate from the girls." He motioned toward the other side of the room. "You're over there, Anthony."

Ant glanced at the kids sitting in his new cluster. "There?" he repeated. Maybe Mr. Reese was directionally challenged. There was no way he was pointing to the right spot.

But nope—he sure 'nuff was. "You got it!" Mr. Reese said, dashing Ant's hopes.

His new seat was smack dab in the middle of three girls—one on each side and one across from him. The only other boy in the cluster was Terrence, a known and certified snitch.

Ant turned back to Jamal. "I guess I'll see you at recess."

"If we even have recess," Mr. Reese added, though no one had asked his opinion. "Looks like it's going to rain."

Ant slogged over to his new group. He knew Rochelle and Layla—they'd all been classmates last year, and they were nice enough. The other girl in their cluster was new. She was almost a head taller than him, with boxy shoulders, high cheekbones, and hair that spiraled in tiny twists around her face.

But he didn't really notice any of that until later. No siree. The first thing he saw was her skin. It was brown.

Mahogany, even.

But as quickly as he noticed it, he reminded himself that he wasn't into girls. No way, no how, no can do. He didn't have time for nonsense like romance.

But *if* he was into girls, then *maybe* he would have considered her cute. Pretty, even.

Of course, the new girl picked that moment to look up from her paper. She and Ant stared at each other for a few seconds.

"Yeah?" she finally asked.

Ant quickly shifted his gaze toward the whiteboard. The girl huffed, then went back to her paper.

Ant chanced another peek. Whatever she was writing, it was long and detailed. She would stop every few words to erase something, only to rewrite it, her pencil pressing even harder into the sheet as a small smile tugged at her lips.

Ant watched as she attacked the paper. Then suddenly a voice broke through his thoughts. "Mr. Reese, I don't think Ant knows the assignment."

Ant looked up. Sure enough, Terrence's hand was straight in the air, like a naked flagpole screaming for attention. Ant wondered if Terrence's arm ever got tired from all the hand raising he did.

Mr. Reese walked over. "Ant? Is that what you prefer to go by?"

Ant quickly nodded.

"Okay, *Annnnnt,*" he said, stretching out the name. Then he clapped his hands. "Let's get started on that letter. Carpe diem, homie."

Ant rolled his eyes.

Rain or shine, recess couldn't get here soon enough.

# CHAPTER 5

The morning seemed to drag on forever. First the class had to watch what felt like one hundred hours of safety videos. Then they had their first group assignment: to come up with a name for their cluster.

Of course, Terrence took the assignment the most seriously—taking notes, and even volunteering a scientific fact to go with every one of their suggestions. (For instance, the Wombats was out—no one needed to know that wombat poop came out looking like a cube.) They finally decided on a name—the Dolphins. Rochelle thought they were cute, Terrence liked that they were intelligent, and Ant, Layla, and Shirley had given up on trying to vote for anything else.

That was the new girl's name—Shirley Heyward. She had moved to South Carolina from Texas that summer.

And like Ant, she didn't care to learn any new and exciting facts about wombat poop. Or dolphin poop. Ant tried not to wonder what else they might have in common as Mr. Reese droned on through a math lesson.

Eventually, recess time rolled around. Except, as Mr. Reese had predicted, it was raining.

"Sorry," he said as he peeked out the window. "Looks like we won't be going outside today."

The class groaned.

"But we can pull out some board games from the closet."

Ant glanced at Jamal across the room as everyone cheered.

"Since this is the first day, I'm going to let you all move around and group up however you like," Mr. Reese said. "But if it gets too loud . . ."

That's all those kids needed to hear. Before Ant knew it, Layla and Rochelle had stood from their desks and were making their way over to a group of girls who had already plopped into a tightly knit circle in the back of the room.

Terrence cleared his throat. "Y'all want to play a game? Maybe Sorry! or Trivial Pursuit? Or—"

"What about spades?" Ant asked. "I've been dying to get a game in."

Terrence shook his head. "I don't know," he began. "Don't we need four players? Plus, I only just learned how to play and I'm not so good yet—"

"Don't worry," Jamal said as he walked over. "We won't beat you too bad." He nodded at Shirley. "Hey, what about you?"

She didn't respond.

"Hey?" he repeated. "Didn't you hear me?"

She finally cut her eyes at him. "I'm not a horse."

"What?"

"I don't respond to *hey*," she said.

"Come on, girl," Jamal said. "I was just—"

"Shirley, this is my best friend, Jamal," Ant said, busting in before Jamal made things worse. "Jamal, Shirley is from Texas."

Now, at that age, some boys didn't give girls the time of day. Others, well, they knew how to crank up the charm. And it wasn't too hard to tell which camp Jamal fell into.

He smiled, and—I kid you not—a brand-new dimple appeared in his cheek.

Height *and* dimples? It didn't seem fair.

"What do you say, *Shirley*?" Jamal said. "You in or what?"

Shirley's demeanor relaxed, but only a little. "I haven't

played in a long time, but sure, I'm in. Does Mr. Reese have cards that we can use?"

"I've already got them," Ant said, pulling the deck out. He took a small amount of comfort in the fact that she turned away from Jamal to look at him when he spoke.

But Shirley frowned, and Ant's happiness turned to muck. "You carry a deck of cards with you?"

"Well," Ant stammered. "Um . . ."

"Technically, they're *my* cards," Jamal said. "Ant's kinda like my caddy."

Now it was Ant cutting his eyes at Jamal.

"We play all the time," Jamal continued. "Not to brag, but we're kind of a big deal."

"They *are* pretty good," Terrence added. "Every year, there's a big spades tournament at the park. Jamal and Ant did *really* well in the tournament last year."

Jamal's grin vanished like the last piece of sweet potato pie at a family reunion. He leaned into Terrence. "What do you mean, *really* well? You trying to be funny, bobblehead?"

Ant was so surprised by the way Jamal scowled at Terrence, he almost dropped the cards.

"No! I just—" Terrence floundered as the words came out of his mouth. "My sister said that Ant won! I just assumed—"

"She must have meant my brother," Ant said. "Come on, let's play already."

But Shirley was staring down Jamal. "Why'd you call him bobblehead?"

"I was kidding," Jamal said, regaining his dimpled smile. "People call him that all the time because of how big his head is—no offense, Terrence." Jamal nodded at Ant. "Kinda like how people call him Ant because he's so little."

Ant glared at Jamal. They'd been friends long enough for Jamal to know that his nickname was short for Anthony. And he had *never* heard anyone call Terrence bobblehead before.

Now, if I were Ant, I would have stood up and knocked Jamal right upside *his* bobblehead. But I guess Ant was more forgiving than me, because he just said, "Yeah. Whatever. *Now* can we get to playing?"

"Okay," Jamal said. "How about . . . first to two hundred, or whoever has the highest score before recess is over wins. Joker-Joker-Deuce. Ten gets you two. Board is four. No points for sandbags. Good?"

Terrence raised his hand, even though he didn't have to. "What does all that even mean?"

"He's just trying to show off," Shirley said. "All you need to remember is that the top cards are the big joker, little joker, and the deuce of spades. I'll take care of everything else."

"You sure you haven't played in a while?" Jamal asked.

She shrugged. "Time is relative."

Ant couldn't help but smile. Shirley was quick on her feet!

The kids rearranged the desks so that Ant and Jamal would be facing each other. Jamal sat to Shirley's left. He started to slouch down in his seat, but one quick glance at Shirley had him straightening up, his back as stiff as an ironing board. She was still taller than him, but it was much less noticeable.

And now they both towered over poor Ant.

Satisfied with his new posture, Jamal grinned at Shirley and said, "Don't worry. I'll go easy on you."

Ant rolled his eyes as he began shuffling the cards. He would have given anything for Erika del Rosario to be in their class right then . . . so Jamal could focus on her instead of Shirley.

Terrence cut the cards, and then Ant began to deal. And then—just so *he* could show off as well—Ant started dealing the cards out of order.

Sure enough, it got Shirley's attention. "What are you doing?"

“Just practicing for the tournament,” Ant said. “Don’t worry—I never misdeal.”

“Hmm. Whatever.” She did not seem impressed.

Once Ant finished dealing, he checked his hand. It was halfway decent. He had:

**SPADES:**
little joker, ace, queen, six, three

**DIAMONDS:**
king, jack

**CLUBS:**
seven, six, three

**HEARTS:**
jack, ten, four

Ant squinted at his cards, memorizing them, before pulling them back into a pile and placing them facedown on this desk. Then he ripped a piece of paper from his notebook. He drew a line down the center of the score sheet, then wrote US at the top of one column, and THEM at the top of the other.

“How you looking, partner?” Shirley asked Terrence. “I’ve got four books and two possibles.”

Terrence frowned at his cards. “I’m not really sure . . .”

"Just do your best," Shirley said. "It's only a game. No one cares if you make a mistake."

"Guess again," Jamal mumbled.

"I've got . . . two. Maybe three," Terrence said.

She put her cards down. "We'll go seven," she told Ant.

Under THEM, Ant wrote 7. "Whatcha got?" he asked Jamal.

The boy grinned across from him. His eyes were wide, and his shoulders bounced. "Man, I got, like, three and a possible."

Ant cocked his head. He figured he could get at least three, and maybe another one depending on how soon he could start cutting diamonds. But where was Jamal counting his books from? Hearts?

He took a breath. "We'll go seven as well."

Jamal winked at Shirley. "I guess that means somebody's about to get set."

# CHAPTER 6

Alright, youngbloods, I know what you're thinking: How do you play spades? What does all that mean? Sandbags? Two hundred? Joker-Joker-Deuce?

Good thing I'm here to break it down for you, so you'll know when Ant's living high on the hog or when he's down in the dumps during a game. Just consider me your all-knowing, *mostly* hands-off observer in the sky. Your play-by-play announcer for this great African American institution called spades.

First of all, spades is typically a four-person game—two teams made up of two players. Partners sit across from each other.

Before they begin playing, the teams decide on the rules. Generally, the house (or the owner of the deck of cards, or even the team who won the previous game) makes the rules. In Ant's case, because they're short on time, they're playing a simplified version of the game. In order to win, a team had to get two hundred—as in, two hundred points. For most teams, you can reach that score in three hands.

There are fifty-two cards in the playing deck—that makes thirteen rounds in a hand, since each round is made up of four cards, and called a book or trick. Once the full deck is dealt, each team tries to guess the number of books they think they'll win. This is called bidding. It's kinda like a contract.

Once the bidding is done and written down on a sheet of paper, each player takes a turn playing a card, with the player to the dealer's left starting first. That first card determines the suit for that round. If you have a card in that suit, you gotta play it, and the highest card wins the book. But if you don't have a card in that suit, you plunk down whatever you've got and prepare to lose.

That is, unless you plop down a spade.

You see, spades are the trump suit. That means they always beat diamonds, hearts, and clubs. The higher the spade, the better the chance it has at winning a book.

In other words:

A ten of hearts beats a four of hearts.

A four of clubs beats a jack of hearts, *if* clubs were the lead suit. If hearts were the lead suit, then the jack would win.

But a three of spades beats a king of diamonds, and a jack of hearts, and a four of clubs, no matter what order the cards are played in.

If you're playing Joker-Joker-Deuce—like Ant is—the highest cards are the big joker, the little joker, and the deuce (or two) of spades, followed by ace, king, queen, jack, ten . . . and so on and so forth.

At the end of the hand, you count up all your books and compare it to your earlier bid. You get ten points for each book bid—but nothing for any books over your bid. (Those are called sandbags, and in the version of the game they're playing, you don't get diddly-squat for 'em.) So to summarize, if Ant and Jamal win seven books, they'll get seventy points. If they win eight books, they'll still get those seventy points.

Now, if you're good, you meet your bid. If you're really good—like Ant and Jamal *think* they are—you meet your bid without taking too many extra books. And if you're *great,* you meet your bid and *set* the other team—meaning, you take so many books they don't meet their bid and earn negative points. In this case, if Shirley and Terrence don't take all seven books they bid, they'll get negative seventy points.

Have you ever eaten a whole bowl of chocolate ice cream, then looked up to see a whole 'nother bowl waiting for you? Without having to eat all the veggies off your dinner plate? That's what it feels like to win a hand and set the other team at the same time. And doing it at the end of a game? Shoot—that's like two bowls of ice cream with sprinkles and hot fudge on top.

Plus, you earn bragging rights until the next time y'all play again. And bragging rights are more valuable than a packet of hot sauce at a fish fry.

But I'm getting ahead of myself.

For now, let's just see if it's Ant's or Shirley's team who's doing the whuppin'. Because both teams bid seven, and since there are only thirteen books in a deck, somebody for sure is about to get set.

# CHAPTER 7

Shirley led off the first hand with an ace of hearts. She knew it was a safe bet—and a card that was almost guaranteed to win a book. You see, that early in the game, the odds were that everyone had at least one card of every suit in their hand.

But then Jamal cut with a four of spades, and all the normal odds went the way of Jheri curls, polyester suits, and eight-track tapes.

Shirley's eyes narrowed. "You don't have any hearts?"

Ant grinned. "Stop harassing my partner and play."

It wasn't exactly the clever trash talk his dad was famous for—the kind that got under an opponent's skin and made 'em slip up—but Ant figured that it was a step in the right direction.

Of course, Jamal didn't have any problem with slinging a little muck. After winning two books in a row, he said, "You know . . . I should change my name to the Library of Congress . . . 'cause I am *full* of books." Then he slapped down the queen of clubs.

Of course, Ant noticed how Shirley smiled at Jamal's comment.

But Ant was also studying the game, and paying attention to who was playing what. By playing that queen of clubs, Ant assumed that Jamal was trying to get rid of that suit. The problem was, the *king* of clubs hadn't been played yet. Ant was pretty sure that Terrence had the card in his hand—the boy had that *"By golly, I'm going to win a book"* look that all rookies wear on their face when they get excited.

So Ant decided to use one of his dad's moves. Before Terrence had a chance to put down his card, Ant pulled out his little joker and held it like he was going to play it next. And of course, Ant held the card just low and turned enough so Terrence could clearly see it.

Terrence glanced at Ant's hand—at that little joker waiting to eat his king of clubs all up—and instead, he decided to play a low club.

Ant smiled, slid the little joker back into his hand, and played the six of clubs.

"But—but—" Terrence began.

"But what?" Jamal asked. "You mad because you were looking all up in my partner's hand and got tricked? If you're too little to run with the big dogs, stay in the doghouse."

"Don't worry about them," Shirley told Terrence. "Just play your cards."

But of course, once Jamal could smell blood in the water, he dialed the trash talk all the way up to one hundred.

"Tell me something, beanstalk," he said to Shirley a few turns later. "Does this card look like a big joker?" He grinned as he placed the card on the table. "Wasn't sure you could see it all the way up there, looking like a giraffe and everything."

Shirley shifted in her seat—maybe even shrank down a bit—but didn't say anything.

"Oh, and by the way—y'all are set," Jamal said.

"Your go, Terrence," Shirley said, staring at her hand.

Terrence tossed out his last spade—an ace.

"Ooooooh," Jamal sang. "That's gotta sting. You should have played that earlier."

Terrence huffed. "I told you I just learned."

"The only thing you learned is how to get your tail whipped!" Jamal said. "You better be glad that Ant and I are rusty. If not, we might have dropped a dime on y'all. Shoot—we may have run a Boston."

"I don't know what that means," Terrence said.

"Who cares who wins?" Shirley said. "We're just playing for fun."

But Ant noticed the bite in her voice. She didn't sound like she was having fun.

"You know, string bean, the only time people say that is when they're losing." Then Jamal outright laughed. "But that is one thing y'all are really good at. Losing!"

Ant shot his friend a look. Jamal had always been a little—what do you young'uns call it . . . *extra*??—when it came to trash talk. But now he was starting to take things a bit too far. Especially on a newbie like Terrence.

Plus, every time Jamal mentioned Shirley's height, she flinched ever so slightly. Nobody else seemed to notice. But Ant did. Then again, he was probably paying too much attention to a girl that he *definitely* didn't like.

By the end of the hand, Ant and Jamal had racked up eight books to the other team's five. Ant wrote down *70* under US and *–70* under THEM.

Terrence began to stand. "Maybe y'all should find someone else to play—"

"Sit down, Terrence," Shirley said. Or actually, more like demanded. "We don't run away just because we lost one little game."

Ant gulped. That comment brought back too many bad memories.

Shirley glanced at the clock as she collected the cards. "But I *am* getting a little bored. So how about this—whoever has the highest score at the end of this next round is the winner?"

Ant checked the score again. There was practically no way that Shirley and Terrence could come back. They were down by 140 points. Ant and Jamal could play it safe on their next bid and still win.

But even though the game was pointless, they could still use the extra reps. "I guess that's okay," Ant said.

Jamal nodded as well. "For real, I promise we won't embarrass y'all as much as we did last time. We'll only win by . . ." Jamal trailed off as he watched Shirley shuffle the cards.

"Uh, what are you doing?" Jamal asked.

Shirley randomly sorted through the cards, moving some to the front and others to the back. "We all aren't fancy shufflers like your *little* partner over there."

"Hey!" Ant said.

"Some of us just have to mix them up any way we can," she said, talking over Ant. "So how *did* y'all do in the tournament last year?"

Ant and Jamal glanced at each other from across the table, neither speaking.

She grinned. "Oh, that bad?"

"It was a fluke," Ant said. "But this year, we're winning it all."

"Yeah. I'm sure you believed that last year, too," Shirley said. "I get it. Sometimes the cards don't fall your way." She locked eyes with Ant. "You guys got the . . . *short* end of the stick."

Whew—that young lady has a tongue sharper than a switchblade. Little—I mean *young* Ant better figure out how to fight back, or he was gonna get carved to bits.

He sat there for a moment with his arms crossed, trying to come up with *something* smart to say. Something that stung. But his mind was as empty as a poor man's bank account.

"I'm almost done," Shirley continued. "I just need a *little* bit longer."

Slice!

"You sure are talking a lot of junk for someone who's losing," Jamal said. "How about y'all put your money where your mouth is."

Ant sat up. "Jamal, I don't think that's a good idea. We shouldn't be betting."

Jamal waved him off. "Don't worry about it. It's not really betting, because they can't really win."

That made Shirley smile. "How about we keep this between me and you?" Shirley said to Jamal. "Ten dollars says that we'll win the next hand, and set y'all, too."

"I'll take that bet," Jamal said. "But don't be complaining later when I take your money."

"Do I look like a crier?" Shirley placed the cards in front of Ant. "Your cut, *shorty*."

Ant slumped back into his seat. For once, he wasn't thinking about Shirley's snide comments. Jamal knew that Ant wasn't supposed to be gambling. It was the one rule that his parents had about playing spades. Shoot—they wouldn't have even let him participate in the tournament if there had been an entry fee. And even though it was Jamal—not Ant—who had made the wager, he wasn't sure his parents would see the difference. But he couldn't exactly run out on his best friend.

After Ant cut the cards, Shirley picked up the deck, then tilted it so she could see the bottom one.

"What are you doing?" Ant asked. "You can't look. That's cheating, Miss . . ." Ant paused, thinking through all the things he could call Shirley. He watched her lips purse and her smooth brown hands tense up as she prepared herself for whatever he was going to say.

He felt himself deflate. "Miss Texas."

"The bottom card is *my* card," she said calmly. "I can look at it anytime I want. Isn't that right, Mr. . . ."

Ant waited for Shirley to take another shot at his height.

"Isn't that right," she repeated, "Mr. Fancy Dealer?"

Ant let out a little breath. *Mr. Fancy Dealer*—that was pretty good. Silly, but not insulting.

"Man, y'all are the corniest trash talkers I've ever played with," Jamal said. "Ant, you'd better up your game before the tournament."

Ant just shrugged. Shirley did, too.

Once she dealt out all the cards, Ant picked up his hand. The highest card he had was a five of hearts.

*A five!!!!*

He checked the score, then glanced at Jamal, whose face had turned as sour as rotten milk.

"Go ahead and bid," Shirley said. "It shouldn't take y'all too long to count all those losing cards in your hand."

"Y'all cheated!" Jamal said, his voice getting loud.

Mr. Reese looked up from his desk. "Is there a problem over there?"

Everyone shook their heads. "No, sir."

But they couldn't just go back to a quiet game of cards. They'd gotten the attention of a few other students. "Y'all are playing spades?" Marco asked. "Who's up?"

"I can't win a single book with my hand," Jamal mumbled.

Shirley leaned back in her seat. "You know what? We'll help Ant and the blabbermouth out, and bid first. Terrence, whatcha got?"

Terrence was still organizing his hand. "I might have four . . . maybe five. Maybe even—"

"Put us down for a dime," Shirley said.

A few kids gasped.

"Wait! How many is that?" Terrence asked.

"It's ten," Shirley said. She ran her thumb against her cards, making a *thwap* sound. "Jamal, I'm not as good as you are with all the fancy lingo, so maybe you could help me out. You did say, 'Ten gets you two.' Right?"

When Jamal didn't answer, Shirley turned to Ant.

"Your partner seems to have lost his voice. Why don't you help him out?"

Ant didn't like the way this was going. Not at all. "Those are the rules we agreed on," he said.

"And just to be clear," Shirley continued, "two stands for two hundred. As in, if we win these ten books, we'll get two hundred *points*."

Ant reluctantly nodded.

Shirley ran her thumb against the cards again. *Thwap. Thwap.* "You know, ten books might be too *low* of a bid. I bet we could run a Boston—"

"Ain't nobody winning all thirteen books up in here," Jamal said. Then he focused on his cards again and scowled.

*Thwap. Thwap. Thwap.* "Naw . . . we'll let y'all get at least one book. Just put us down for the dime. Then go ahead and bid board for yourself."

"What does that mean?" Terrence asked.

"The board is the lowest number of books a team can bid—four," Shirley said. Then she looked at Ant. "Well, what are you waiting on? Write it down. We don't have all day."

Ant grumbled . . . then wrote down 10 in her team's column and 4 in his.

Five minutes and twelve rounds later, Shirley and

Terrence hadn't lost a book. What was worse, almost everyone in the class had come over to watch the game, oohing and aahing with each card Shirley and Terrence collected.

Shucks—by the end of it, even Mr. Reese was paying attention.

"And just 'cause we're feeling generous," Shirley said to Jamal after playing a card, "I'll let you win this last book with that jack of hearts you've been holding on to."

Jamal grimaced . . . and did exactly as she said.

"How did you know what he had?" Terrence asked. "Are you psychic?"

"Okay, that was fun, but let's get ready for science," Mr. Reese said, walking toward his desk.

Some students began to drift toward their clusters, but not Marco. "Hold up," he said to Shirley. "You *gotta* make 'em sign the paper."

That was the thing about spades—if you were beat that badly, you were supposed to sign your names to the score—a semipermanent reminder of just how bad you got whupped.

Shirley pulled a pen from her desk. "Use this. I don't want it to fade."

"I can't believe they just dropped a dime on Jamal and

Ant," Layla whispered to Rochelle as Ant took the pen from Shirley.

"Well, they aren't *that* good," Rochelle replied. "Don't you know what happened last year . . . ?"

Apparently, that was enough for Jamal, because he stood up before Ant could sign. "This game doesn't count," he said. "You cheated."

And then he stormed off.

Shirley shrugged. "No sweat. I'll just get his signature when I collect my payment."

# CHAPTER 8

For the rest of the day, Ant waited for Shirley to crack a joke about how badly he and Jamal had lost. But surprisingly, she never did. If the shoe had been on the other foot, he wasn't sure he and Jamal would have been able to stop themselves from gloating.

Then again, Shirley didn't have to trash-talk—her skills spoke for themselves.

As bad as the thumping had been, Ant began to feel better about it as the day went on. By lunch, he'd even stopped wanting to hide in the bathroom. Plus, the loss made Ant realize that he and Jamal had a lot of practicing to do before the tournament.

And that's exactly what he planned to tell Jamal once class was over. Except Jamal didn't wait for Ant after the final bell rung. He was out the door before Ant had even zipped up his backpack.

"He must be really scared that I'm going to ask for that money," Shirley said. "You can tell him that I was just playing."

Ant picked up his backpack. "Jamal's serious about spades."

"Yeah, and water is wet." She must have noticed the confused look on Ant's face, because she added, "Duh, of course he's hard-core about it. But so are you—flashing that little joker so Terrence would play something else. That was a really smart move, pulling the peekaboo."

"The peekaboo! That's what my dad calls it."

"Your dad taught you to play spades?"

Ant nodded. "Yep!"

Shirley smiled as she rose from her seat. "Well, maybe you'd better get a few more pointers from him." There was the zinger Ant had been waiting for. As Shirley started toward the door, Ant began to question if he'd made a mistake in laying off her. But then she turned around long enough to say, "See you tomorrow . . . Ant."

Poor youngblood's heart began to flutter something awful. He didn't even know why. All he knew was, Shirley hadn't called him little.

She had actually spoken his name.

And she just might have been smiling when she said it.

Ant found Jamal waiting for him outside. "Dude, were you really worried that she was going to ask for her money?"

Jamal started walking. "Naw, man. It was the guys in my cluster. They kept nagging me for the rest of the day—snickering and stuff. All because we lost to Terrence and that dumb girl."

There were a lot of things that Jamal could say about Shirley, but being dumb wasn't one of them. Ant stared straight ahead. "The way you were going on, I thought you *liked* that *dumb* girl."

"I thought she was kinda cute, at first. But she talks too much. Way too much mouth."

"In other words . . . she's like you?"

Jamal frowned. "Man, it's okay for boys to play around like that. Like, it's in our DNA. But nobody likes it when a girl talks trash." Jamal arched an eyebrow. "Don't think I didn't notice how *you* were staring at her. Maybe you should step to her? Ask her for her number?"

Ant's eyes bugged out of his head. "What? Me? No!"

Jamal cackled. "Little Ant, still scared to talk to girls."

"What's with you and all the *little* stuff," Ant said. "Lay off, okay?"

"Come on, Ant. It's just a joke. Don't be so sensitive."

Ant couldn't help but notice how it was "just a joke" when Jamal said stuff, but Shirley was a "dumb girl" when she did the same.

"You want to go over to the Quick Mart and register for the tournament today?" Ant asked once they crossed the street. "Then we can practice at my house. Dad promised to play when he gets home from work."

"Why the rush? It's not like they're gonna run out of space."

Unlike the teen and adult tournaments, the junior division only ever had a handful of teams sign up. Which, in a way, made it worse that Ant and Jamal had been bounced so early last year. Still, Ant wanted to register early . . . and maybe take a peek at who else had already signed up. Size up the competition.

"I just hope they bumped up the prize money," Jamal continued. "I mean, one hundred dollars is nice, but I want that big money, like in the other divisions."

Ant shrugged. He knew he was supposed to care about money, but it had never been the reason he played. "So are we going or not?" Ant asked. "Or do you need to ask your mom first?"

"She won't care," Jamal said, bending down to pull a rock from his shoe.

"Man, you'd better call your momma. Or at least your aunt Rebbie. The last time you came over and didn't tell anyone, your mom threatened to—"

"Just drop it, alright?!" Jamal chucked the pebble into the road. "Rebbie's probably on her way to work, and Ma's . . . tied up." Jamal pushed past Ant and powered down the street. "You coming or what?"

Hmm . . . *now* who was being sensitive?

# CHAPTER 9

The Connally Quick Mart was practically a historic landmark, at least to the residents of Oak Grove. It was one of the first Black-owned businesses in the city, opened by Rose Connally back before Ant's granddaddy could even hold a single card, let alone a full deck. For the past fifty-one years, the store had been run by Rose's son, Eugene. The Quick Mart was a place where old folks and youngbloods alike could buy the necessities, see a friendly face, and get the latest gossip. A real neighborhood joint. And it was Eugene who first devised the Oak Grove Labor Day Festival—and its infamous Spades Tournament.

You see, unlike the other events at the park, the Labor Day Festival wasn't an official, city-sponsored event. Eugene was the one who filled out all the permits, organized all the vendors, and rounded up all the corporate donations. He worked hard to make it as inexpensive as possible so everyone could attend.

"Ah, Ant and Jamal—me and the boys were wondering when y'all were gonna show up." Mr. Eugene sat on a large stool at his usual spot behind the cash register. A few feet away, the "boys"—three old-timers named Casey, Ellis, and Selmon—played dominoes on a small table. Every time Ant entered the store, he found those same men in those same spots, each holding on to their dominoes like a vulture clutches its roadkill. Ant had stopped wondering if the men actually purchased anything and just accepted that they were as much a part of the place as the jars of pickled pig feet lining the shelves or the ancient rusted fan that was always spinning on high.

"Hey there, ankle biter," Mr. Casey said, nodding at Ant. The man didn't have a lot of hair on his head, but he made up for it with the hair coming out of his nose and ears. "So y'all gonna actually win this year? Or go running off with your tail between your legs again?"

"Be quiet, fool," Mr. Selmon said, nudging Mr. Casey on the shoulder. "You ain't supposed to say stuff like that out loud."

"They just had the jitters," Mr. Ellis added without

looking up from the domino pieces on the table. "Ain't that right, fellas?"

Jamal puffed out his chest. "*I* didn't cry. *I* took my loss like a man."

Of course, that caused everyone to turn to Ant.

"Don't pay them no mind," Mr. Eugene said as he pulled a beat-up notebook from underneath the counter. "Shoot—Jordan didn't win on his first try in the playoffs. Neither did LeBron."

"But Magic did," Mr. Casey said.

"We'll do better this year," Jamal said. "I mean, there's no way that Ant can mess up and renege again."

Reneging was the biggest sin you could commit in spades. It was when you played a card—usually a spade—out of suit, when you still had a card from the lead suit in your hand. Last year, Ant had plunked down a spade to beat a jack of hearts, when he still had a ten of hearts to play. And he hadn't stopped kicking himself about it since.

Now, Ant didn't appreciate the commentary from Jamal, but he kept his mouth shut. Right or wrong, he wasn't about to throw his partner under the bus.

Never mind that Jamal had overbid.

Never mind that they were about to lose anyway.

Never mind that Jamal had suggested that they renege if they got into trouble.

Their loss was clearly all Ant's fault.

And maybe it was. At the end of the day, *he* was the one who had broken the rules. So maybe it was only fair that he received the brunt of the trash talk when the other team discovered his mistake.

Mr. Eugene pointed to the rear of the store by the old video poker machine. "Jamal, go on to the back and grab me a pack of peanut M&M's."

"But why should I . . . ?"

Jamal stopped talking as the old-timers directed their gaze onto *him*. Those men might have been elderly, but they were still OGs and were *not* to be trifled with.

Jamal groaned. "One pack of peanut M&M's, coming up."

Mr. Eugene nodded toward Ant once Jamal was gone. "Hold your head up, son," he said softly. "I still believe in you."

"Thanks, Mr. Eugene."

"And tell your daddy to give me a call," he said. "I've been trying to get ahold of that fella all afternoon. Got a question about my returns."

"Sure thing, Mr. Eugene," Ant said. "Dad's supposed to be home early today."

Jamal returned with the bag of candy. "Here you go."

Mr. Eugene coughed—followed by hacks from Ellis, Selmon, and Casey—as they all eyed Jamal.

Jamal sighed. "I mean, here you go, *sir.*"

"That's better," Mr. Eugene said, his throat suddenly free and clear. Then he frowned. "Boy, weren't you listening? You know I can't eat peanuts. I'd be clogged up for a week. Get me the Kit Kat like I asked."

"But you said—" Jamal turned back around. "Yes, sir."

The men at the domino table broke into a fit of laughter as Jamal trudged off again. Mr. Eugene winked at Ant. "So what should I ask for next, slick? A Twix or Peppermint Pattie?"

# CHAPTER 10

Luckily for Jamal, Mr. Eugene finally laid off long enough for the boys to sign up for the tournament. Then they headed home, but not before wolfing down the half-price pack of M&M's that Mr. Eugene had sold them.

Of course, my man Ant didn't know that Eugene had only given it to them for a discount because the bag had expired two months ago. But hey—there were worse secrets being kept from Ant.

Ant's mother was already out of her work scrubs by the time the boys got there.

Ant's father, however, was still out. And he hadn't arrived by four o'clock. Or five. Or even six. Ant and Jamal sat at the kitchen table fiddling with the deck of cards, but not really playing with them. Spades was a game for four, not two or three, so practicing for the tournament was on hold until Ant's dad showed up.

"I don't know what's taking Roland so long," Ant's mother said. "Jamal, you're welcome to stay over for dinner."

Jamal looked down at the table. "Thank you, but I'd better head home."

"Well, you're more than welcome to come over. Anytime." She paused extra long after she said this. "And tell Rebbie that goes for the rest of the family as well."

Jamal quickly nodded. "Thank you, Mrs. Joplin."

Ant waited until his friend was gone before asking, "Is something going on with Jamal's mom?"

"You're way too perceptive for your own good." She opened the refrigerator and peered inside. "How about spaghetti for dinner? Not that you have a choice, mind you."

"Then I guess it sounds great," Ant said. Spaghetti was one of his mother's safer meals. "But you didn't answer my question. I know something is up. Jamal shut down earlier when I mentioned his mom. Is she using again?"

His mother pulled out a package of hamburger meat and brought it to the stove. "No one really knows for sure.

She did take off again, though. They haven't seen or heard from her in a month." Yolanda studied her son. "I'm guessing Jamal didn't tell you."

Ant followed her to the counter. "Not a word."

Ant had known Jamal and his family for most of his life. Jamal's momma was a bit on the wild side. Couldn't keep a steady job or home, and had a bad habit of picking the absolutely worst boyfriends. Jamal and his seventeen-year-old brother, Taj, lived with their aunt Rebbie's family. Their mom had been staying with them—and it had looked like she was finally turning her life around. But bad habits can be hard to break.

"He'll talk to you about it when he's ready. That poor boy likes to keep things bottled up. And speaking of people who hold things in . . ." She glanced at her cell, sitting on the counter by her purse and hospital ID badge. "Maybe I should call your father."

"I'll do it," Ant said as he reached for his phone.

"Just don't ask about work," his mother warned. "He might not want to talk about it."

Ant called his father, but the line just rang and rang. He hung up after the call went to voice mail. A few seconds later, his father texted, **Sorry, buddy. Tied up in a meeting. Will be home late tonight.**

"What did he say?" his mother asked, the creases carved into her forehead.

"He's still working," Ant repeated flatly. "He says he'll be home later."

"Hmm . . . that pitch to Jerry Monroe shouldn't have taken this long." She checked the clock.

"Are you worried?"

She quickly shook her head. "No. Of course not. This is probably a good sign."

Ant wasn't sure who she was trying to convince—him or herself.

# CHAPTER 11

Ant had a hard time sleeping that night. He kept tossing and turning, shadowboxing with his sheets. Not-so-good thoughts about his father kept bubbling up. He hadn't come home by the time Ant had gone to bed. He hadn't even called. And when Ant *did* drift off, his dreams were full of images that made his neck sweat. Playing in the tournament last year. Losing book after book, hand after hand. Everyone from the neighborhood watching him choke. Whispers giving way to roaring laughter.

And then the worst image of all—Ant tearing away from the card table with tears streaming down his face.

It wasn't that he lost, it was that he cracked under pressure. Ant turned tail and ran away. Like a little kid.

And that just won't do.

Now, I know Ant's father has been trying to encourage him to be tougher. To be more like him. Like Aaron. Like a real Joplin man.

But Ant? Youngblood is still a work in progress.

Eventually, night turned into morning, and soon the lights in Ant's room started flicking on and off in silent alarm.

"Rise and shine, Ant!" his father boomed from the doorway.

Ant jolted awake. "I'm up, I'm up," he said, rubbing his eyes.

"Get on out of bed and get dressed," Ant's dad said as the light switch came to rest in the on position. "Your mother's already left for work, and I've got to get out of here early this morning, which means I need to make sure you're ready to leave before I go."

"I can handle getting myself to school," Ant said.

"Take that up with your mother tonight. She says you can't be left alone, and apparently, *she's* the boss around here." His father chuckled. "I guess it's good that I make a mean bowl of Cocoa Pebbles."

Ant knew that his dad was joking, but the edge in his voice didn't feel very funny. At least he was smiling as he left Ant to do his business.

Ant quickly splashed some water on his face and under his arms, then got dressed. He entered the kitchen to find that his father had already poured milk into his bowl, and now the cereal was a mushy mess.

"So how was the first day of school?" his father asked.

"Okay, I guess." He shoveled a spoonful of cereal into his mouth. "Did you know about Jamal's mom?"

"I heard about it last week from the fellas at the Quick Mart," his father said while stirring his coffee. "It's a shame, too. Some people just aren't strong enough to overcome their demons."

"I just wish Jamal had told me," Ant said. "He's supposed to be my best friend."

"Son, some young men aren't wired to do a lot of talking. But Jamal's a strong kid. He can handle it." Roland picked up his mug. "You know, you could learn something from that. Mitchell will be tough. You gotta play the cards you're dealt. You can't run off and cry if you don't like the deal."

"I know," Ant said quickly. Then, hoping to shift gears, he added, "Mr. Eugene is looking for you. He tried to call you, but—"

"I'll follow up with him," his dad said. He drank some

coffee, then returned the mug to the table with a soft thud. "Look, son. I'm not trying to pick on you. I'm just trying to prepare you. Okay?" He playfully punched Ant's shoulder. "Take it from me—the world out there is rough. You gotta learn how to win when the deck's stacked against you." His father paused to wink. "What do you think your momma would say about all those card references?"

That made Ant laugh a little.

"Ah, there you go. Us Joplin men are too pretty to be frowning all the time." He checked his watch. "You sure you're gonna be okay once I leave? You're not going to burn down the house or anything like that once I'm out the door?"

"Dad . . ."

"Well, I guess you made it to school and back yesterday," he said. "But it wasn't that long ago that me and your momma had to drag you there."

"I was in kindergarten."

"I bet I still have marks from where your fingernails dug into my skin."

Ant had heard this story hundreds of times, but it still made him laugh. His dad always found ways to change it up.

"I swear, you were holding on to me like your name was Rose and I was a door floating in the Atlantic . . ."

"Boo to the *Titanic* reference, Dad."

"Like you were Will Smith trying to get jiggy with my leg. Like you were a baby goat and my leg was its mama's—"

"Dad!"

His father leaned back and let out a grizzly-bear-sized laugh. "What? It's true."

Now, to Ant, *this* seemed normal. These were the type of jokes that he liked. Not jokes about his mom's morning shifts. Or Ant not being tough enough.

Once his father stopped laughing, he took another sip from his mug. "Also, I'm sorry about not getting home earlier last night. Something came up."

"Did everything go okay with Mr. Monroe?"

His father gave a half-hearted shrug. "A slight setback, but nothing a Joplin can't handle. I promise—I'll practice with you and Jamal this week. Gonna do my best to get you boys ready for the game."

"We could use all the help we can get," Ant said. "We played yesterday at school. It didn't go so well."

His father raised an eyebrow. "At least you didn't bolt when you lost, right?"

Ant hated that this was the only thing his dad seemed to be worried about. "No, Dad," Ant said. "It happened during class."

"Just remember—how you lose is just as important as how you win," he said. "No sniffling and running off." Then he leaned closer to Ant. "How bad was it?"

"We got a dime dropped on us."

"They beat you like you stole something, huh?" His father grunted. "Well, y'all better not let that happen in the tournament. Can't have y'all sullying my good name." He stood up. "You sure those fellas didn't swindle you?"

"They got a lucky break," Ant said. He was about to add that it had been a girl who beat them, but right or wrong, he couldn't bring himself to say it. He didn't know if getting beat by a girl would make a difference to his father, but his pride couldn't take that chance.

"They were *lucky*?" His father finished the rest of his coffee. "Don't forget, son—we're Joplin men. We make our own luck."

# CHAPTER 12

*We make our own luck.*

Those words rattled around in Ant's head all the way to school. Yesterday, Jamal had claimed that Shirley had cheated by rigging the deck. But maybe she'd just been taking advantage of the situation. Exploiting Jamal and Ant's weakness.

Making her own luck.

Shirley had done some pretty amazing things during the game—like beating Ant and Jamal with a partner who barely knew how to play. And predicting the last card in Jamal's hand. She was as smart a card player as he'd ever seen at their age. Maybe even smarter than he was.

Ant began to wonder, if he asked nicely enough,

whether she might be willing to teach them some tricks. Help them get ready for the tournament.

The way he figured it, Shirley was new to town. She needed friends. Maybe Ant and Jamal could *be* those friends. And then she'd be happy to help them.

Of course, wanting to spend more time with Shirley had absolutely, positively nothing to do with it. He didn't care in the least about how she smiled and talked and laughed and everything else about her that made the boy's skin tingle.

Hmm . . . maybe his daddy should have given him The Talk the other morning after all.

Anyway, he planned to go over his idea with Jamal that morning, but Ant couldn't find him on the playground.

He still wasn't there when the final bell rang, starting the school day.

"Okay, everyone get settled," Mr. Reese said as Ant sank into his seat. "Do you all remember the form you filled out for me over the summer, where I asked you to list some interesting facts about yourself? Well, I used that to create a fun game I like to call Classroom Bingo. Each square contains a fact about one of your classmates. I want you to quietly walk around and interview one another to see who matches each fact, and then write their name down in the box next to it. The student who completes all the squares first wins."

Dwayne, a boy in Jamal's cluster, raised his hand. "What do you get if you win?"

Mr. Reese smiled. "You get the satisfaction of completing an assignment."

Dwayne groaned.

So did Ant. And Shirley. And all of the other kids, except Terrence, whose hand shot into the sky.

"Yes, Terrence?"

"Technically, since this is called *bingo,* shouldn't we only have to complete five squares down or across or diagonally instead of filling out the entire—"

"Good point," Mr. Reese said. "I'll change the name of the game next year." He took a deep breath. "The point of the game isn't to race from person to person. Take your time. Really get to know your classmates. Ask follow-up questions." He clasped his hands together, and Ant didn't know if he was doing it because he was happy or because he was trying to pray. "Come up and talk to me if you have any other questions. Otherwise, get to it!"

Layla and Rochelle went over to Marco and Yvonne's cluster while Terrence zipped toward Mr. Reese, arm raised. But Ant and Shirley remained at their desks.

Ant scanned the sheet, wondering if he could find a good fact to ask Shirley about—something that would hopefully open the door to him talking about spades. But what?

"Have you ever visited Japan?"

He looked up to see Shirley staring at him. It hadn't crossed his mind that she was trying to find something to ask *him* about.

"Well?"

Ant blinked. "Oh. Sorry, no. What about you?"

"I used to live in Germany, but that's not on this sheet."

And just like that, Ant saw his opening. "So is that where you learned how to stack the deck?"

"Are you still mad about that?"

"No! I'm not mad at all. I'm *impressed*." Ant licked his too-dry lips. "I was actually wondering if you'd teach me how you did it."

She smirked. "Sorry, family secret."

"But—"

"Plus, there's no way Jamal wants my help."

"That's not true," Ant said. "I'm sure . . ."

"It's okay," Shirley said. "I don't like helping bullies anyway."

"He's not a bully!"

Shirley crossed her arms. "Really, *little* Ant?"

"He was just . . . It was just—"

"If it makes you feel better, I won't joke about your height anymore." Then her gaze dropped. "Especially since you didn't make fun of mine. Okay?"

Ant slowly nodded. "Okay."

"Good." She rose from her seat. "Now who in here takes ballet?"

Ant watched as Shirley walked off in search of her answer. He rose, knowing he needed to get started on the assignment, too. He kept looking in Shirley's direction, though, hoping to talk to her more. First she interviewed Dwayne, then Terrence, then Katrina. And soon they were on opposite sides of the room.

But that was one good thing about Shirley being so tall, he realized. No matter where she was, she always stood out.

# CHAPTER 13

Just as everyone was finishing Classroom Bingo, Jamal strolled into class. Ant tried to get his attention as he settled into his seat, but Jamal didn't wave back.

But at least it wasn't raining. They could finally go outside for recess.

Ant ran up to Jamal as soon as they were let loose on the playground. "Hey! Where were you this morning?"

"Overslept," Jamal said. "The babies were up all night, and I didn't go to sleep until like four in the morning."

"Oh man. I'm sorry." Ant waited to see if Jamal would say something about how his mom had left, but Jamal didn't seem interested in talking about that. Instead, he pulled a deck of cards from his pocket.

"I was hoping you brought those," Ant said with a

grin. "We need practice if we're going to be ready."

"Yeah, I was thinking about that," Jamal said. "I was talking to my brother about what happened yesterday. I mean, I didn't tell him that we lost to a girl—he'd never let me live that down—but I did tell Taj that we were rusty." He took a deep breath. "We need to talk about signals again."

"Jamal . . ." Signals, like scratching your nose to tell your partner you wanted them to play diamonds or coughing when you wanted clubs, were against the rules.

"All the good teams do it. Ask your brother."

That was the thing. Ant didn't *want* to ask his brother—because he didn't want to know if Aaron cheated as well. That would have made it okay. And Ant didn't want it to be okay.

"I'll be honest," Jamal continued. "I could really use the money. Things are . . . stressed at the house."

"Really? What's going on?" Ant asked.

"Oh. Nothing major," Jamal said, backing away from Ant. "So look, Taj taught me some signals that he uses. I think they could work. Maybe for hearts, we could—"

"Hey, Jamal! Ant!" RJ yelled, rushing over with a football in his hand. "We're down a guy. One of y'all want to play?"

Jamal did his best to cover the cards with his hand. "Thanks, but we're good."

But RJ had already seen the deck. "What? Y'all brought cards outside to recess? Man, that whipping y'all got yesterday wasn't enough?" He turned toward a group of boys a few feet away. "Cordell, how much did Jamal and Ant lose by again? Five hundred points? To Terrence . . . and a girl?"

"They got lucky," Jamal said.

"Or y'all are just bad," RJ countered. "But hey—y'all are used to losing, right?"

RJ and Cordell were fifth graders like Ant, but they were in a different class. And unlike Ant and Jamal, they had *won* their first game in last year's tournament. To be fair, they got blown out in the very next game. But that didn't stop them from gloating.

"Come on, RJ," Cordell said, jogging over to them. "You gonna play football or what?"

"I was trying to find another player," RJ said. "Though I guess if these fools can't beat a girl playing spades, there's no way they should be holding a football."

"It's not like y'all made it very far in the tournament," Ant said. "Losing is losing."

"But we didn't lose to a girl," RJ said.

"Well, at least girls want to talk to us," Jamal snapped back. "With the way your breath smells, you'd have to pay them to give you any attention."

RJ snorted. "That's not what yo mama said last night."

Now, that was pretty watered down when it came to "Yo Mama" jokes, but still, a few of the kids who'd stopped to check out the argument laughed. Ant spotted Shirley hanging out at the back of the crowd, towering over everyone else as she watched them.

Jamal wasn't in a laughing mood. "What did you say about my mom?" he asked, his face now a solid as stone.

Everyone froze. Then came the sound that warned things had gotten *real*. "*Oooooooooh . . .*"

RJ held his hands up. "Jamal . . . dude . . . I was just joking."

Ant grabbed Jamal's arm. "Come on, man. Let's go."

Jamal let out a long breath, and Ant thought everything was good.

But then some knucklehead popped off and hollered, "Dang, Jamal! You gonna let him talk about your momma like that?"

Jamal stood there for a second, processing the challenge. Then he ripped himself out of Ant's grip and charged straight at RJ.

RJ tried to run, but Jamal caught him before he could get away. He flung RJ to the ground, then jumped on top of him.

"FIGHT!" someone yelled.

Ant started toward the boys, hoping to pull Jamal away. But with all the arms and fists flying around, he didn't know how to help without getting knocked around himself. A second later, Cordell launched himself into the pile to separate them, doing what Ant had been too afraid to do.

Once Cordell had created some distance between the boys, Ant grabbed Jamal and pulled him to his feet.

"You better keep my momma's name out of your mouth!" Jamal yelled at RJ. His eyes were wide and his nostrils flared. Ant had never seen him like this before.

"What's wrong with you?" Ant yelled, struggling to keep Jamal in one spot.

Jamal charged again, and it took every ounce of strength in Ant's scrawny little legs to stop Jamal from twisting around him. And then someone was pulling at Jamal. And then at Ant!

He looked up to see Mr. Reese with a firm grip on his arm. "Settle down, Ant."

Mr. Reese's sky-blue eyes were dead serious. He let Ant

go after staring him down for a few seconds. But not Jamal.

Ant turned to see another teacher towering over RJ and Cordell. RJ's lip was busted, but he wasn't trying to fight anymore. Although now that Ant thought about it, he wasn't really sure if RJ had actually tried to fight at all, or if he'd only been protecting himself.

"Let's go," Mr. Reese said. "Everyone to the office."

"But—" all four boys started at the same time.

"Office," the teacher commanded. "Now."

As Ant followed Mr. Reese, he noticed Jamal's playing cards strewn all across the grass. Some of them were bent and others torn—it probably happened during the fight. He considered asking one of his classmates to collect them, then decided against it. What was the point?

He had the feeling that he wouldn't be playing spades with Jamal anytime soon.

# CHAPTER 14

Ant squirmed in the chair outside of Assistant Principal Booker's office. He leaned closer to the door, hoping to hear what she was saying to Cordell, but the fancy noise machine in the corner of the hallway drowned out anything they might have been saying.

He sighed and shifted in his seat again. The fake-leather lime-green cushion was hard and rubbery, kinda like his momma's cube steak, and it squeaked every time he moved.

Ant wondered if Mrs. Booker had picked those chairs on purpose—to make kids as uncomfortable as possible before venturing into her office. But even if that was true, he'd for sure rather be where he was than farther down the hallway talking to Principal Knight—like RJ and Jamal were. Ant could hear Dr. Knight's booming voice all the way from his office.

Clearly, they needed to upgrade them fancy white noise machines.

After a few moments, Mrs. Booker's door opened, and Cordell stepped out. He didn't look at Ant as he shuffled past.

"Come on in, Mr. Joplin," Mrs. Booker called from her desk.

She didn't stand up as Ant entered the room. Her desk was bare, except for a small laptop and a couple pens. Ant wondered—why have pens on your desk if you don't have anything to write on?

"How about we start with you telling me what happened from your point of view?" Mrs. Booker began as Ant settled into yet another fake-leather lime-green seat. "And don't leave anything out."

Now, Ant was a loyal friend, but he wasn't a fool. He was not about to sit there and lie to that woman. So he told her about what had gone down. Maybe he added a little oomph to the part when RJ was talking trash to his friend, but all in all, he told the truth.

Once he'd finished, Mrs. Booker folded her hands on her desk. "And what did *you* do wrong today?"

Ant blinked. *Nothing* was what he wanted to say. But Mrs. Booker wouldn't have been asking that question unless she saw things differently.

Ant thought about it, but he must have taken too long, because Mrs. Booker let out a small, disapproving *tsk* and said, "You shouldn't have tried to stop your friends from fighting."

Ain't that something? The boy didn't even jump into the fracas, and he was still being blamed.

"Well? What do you have to say to that, Mr. Joplin?"

"Technically—just to be clear, ma'am—*Jamal's* my friend. RJ's just a kid I know. And it wasn't like I was fighting. I was trying to hold Jamal back. What was I supposed to do?"

"You were *supposed* to find a teacher." Mrs. Booker picked up one of her pens and twirled it between her fingers. Maybe that's why she kept them on her desk—for digit calisthenics. "And what else could you have done differently?"

"There's more?" Ant asked.

She nodded solemnly. "You shouldn't have been talking so negatively about your friend—or as you said, 'a kid you know.'" She made air quotes as she said the words. "That's not what we're about here at Gerald Elementary."

"But I wasn't the one who—" Ant stopped. Jamal was already in trouble as it was—no need to pour more gasoline on the fire by trying to make himself look better. "It was just innocent trash talk," he said, correcting himself.

"So 'innocent' Jamal decided to body-slam 'a kid you know'?" Mrs. Booker was really digging those air quotes. "What would your mother say if she heard y'all talking like that?"

*Low blow, bringing my mom into it,* Ant thought.

The assistant principal turned toward her computer. "Since you and your friends like to talk so much trash about spades, no one will be playing cards at school for the next nine weeks." Mrs. Booker began typing. "And of course, I'll be calling your parents."

Ant thought about speaking up, but one look from Mrs. Booker made him reconsider. "And before you ask, I'm not treating you special just because your mother and I grew up together. I'll be calling Cordell's parents as well."

"Um . . . thank you?"

Mrs. Booker opened a desk drawer and pulled out a stack of hall passes. "The next time you're in here, I want it to be for a good reason, okay? Not some nonsense like this."

Well, that was one thing they could agree on.

She handed him a pass. "By the way, how's your brother?"

"Aaron texted yesterday. He's good."

Mrs. Booker smiled, finally looking just a little like the woman in his mom's pictures. "Did he take his flute up there with him?"

"There was no way he was leaving here without it. Even though he's not at Mitchell for performing arts, he can still play in the band."

"Good for him," she said. "Y'all will have to let me know if they hold any concerts. I miss hearing him play."

Okay, so maybe they had *two* things they could agree on.

# CHAPTER 15

All things considered, the rest of Ant's day went pretty smoothly. But Jamal never returned to class—an office aide came to collect his backpack. Ant hoped that Jamal had only been issued a day or two of in-school suspension, though he had a sneaking suspicion that it was much, much worse. The thought made his stomach churn.

After school, he found Cordell by the bike rack. Cordell looked worried for a second, like he almost expected Ant to start something. But Ant held up his hands. "I'm not here to argue. I just wanted to see if you knew what happened to RJ and Jamal."

Cordell bent down to pull a chain from between the spokes of his tire. "Word is, Dr. Knight suspended them."

"That's what I was afraid of." Ant sighed. "By the way, thanks for trying to break it up."

"RJ shouldn't have said anything about Jamal's mom." Cordell started wheeling his bike away. "But Jamal still shouldn't have hit him."

"I know."

He gave Ant a quick head nod. "Sorry, but I gotta jet. Have to talk to my mom before she gets that phone call from Mrs. Booker."

"Good idea," Ant said. "Catch you tomorrow."

Ant started off for home, his gaze glued to the top of his brand-new Vans. With the grass stains and mud crusted all over them, they didn't look so pristine anymore. But Ant refused to feel bad about a dumb pair of sneakers. He'd lost something *way* worse.

Knowing Rebbie, Jamal's suspension would probably lead to a three-month grounding.

No video games. No TV. No cell phone.

And for sure, no spades tournament.

So now what was he supposed to do?

When Ant got home, his mom's blue SUV was already under the carport. Had Mrs. Booker called his mom at work?

Shoot—Ant might not be able to play in the tournament, either.

He tentatively placed his hand on the hood. It was still warm. Ant's dad had surprised her with the new SUV last Christmas—before his business started drying up. Prior to that, she'd been driving a beat-up Honda Civic. She loved complaining about the new vehicle—how it was too big for her. But Roland said that she looked too beautiful behind the wheel to return it. And that was true as well.

Ant opened the door to find his mother standing in the center of the kitchen, her back to him and her cell phone pressed against her ear. As soon as the door creaked, she spun around.

Her eyes were wide. Excited. Expectant.

And then they fell.

But Yolanda didn't look angry. She looked like she'd been hoping for a different friendly face to saunter through that door.

She shook the anxiety away and wiggled her pointer finger at Ant—a small hello she reserved just for him. And then, speaking into the phone, she said, "No, I'm glad you called. I'm sure it's nothing. But, yes . . . I'll call or text you as soon as he gets home."

His mother spent the next two minutes trying to

finagle a goodbye out of the person on other end of the line before hanging up.

"Is something wrong?" Ant asked.

"Oh, no," his mother said, placing the phone on the table. "Not really."

Then she sighed.

"C'mon, Ma. What happened?"

She opened her mouth after what felt like an hour of silence, but before she could speak, her phone rang. Ant clocked that same expectant look on her face as she snatched it up off the table. But this time, her excitement was replaced with confusion. "Why is the school calling?"

"Ma, I—"

Too late. She was already answering. "Hello? Oh, hey, Anita. What's up, girl?" His mother's gaze settled on Ant. "I see. Playing cards? And a *fight*?"

Ant took a step backward.

"Anita, I can assure you, nothing like this will *ever* happen again. Thank you for calling. See you at the next sorority meeting."

She ended the call. "There something you want to tell me, Anthony?"

"It wasn't my fault!"

"Do I look like Boo Boo the Fool? How about you try that again?"

So Ant started all the way at the beginning. His mother listened patiently, nodding at Ant, while also sneaking peeks at the blank screen on her phone. She finally snapped to attention when Ant got to the part about Jamal tackling RJ.

"And were you talking trash, too?"

Ant scrunched up his nose. "Well . . . a little. But not nearly as bad as Jamal."

"A little goes a long way, Anthony. As your granddaddy used to say, one day you're gonna write a check that your butt can't cash."

"But it wasn't my fault! Jamal was the one doing all of the fighting. I was trying to stop him."

"Next time, find a teacher." She spun her phone on the tabletop. "Listen, we'll discuss this fight business later. For now, do you want to go on to your room and start your homework before dinner?"

Ant grinned as something that his brother used to pull popped into his head.

"What?" his mother asked.

He knew he should probably keep his mouth shut, but . . .

"Not to be all technical, but if you're *asking* me if I want to do my homework, am I allowed to say no?" he teased.

"Fine, Mr. Smarty-pants. That was a command, not a question." Then she winked. "Now go."

Ant went to his room and pulled his writing notebook from his backpack. Mr. Reese had assigned a personal essay based on the book they'd started reading that morning, *Bud, Not Buddy*. Except before he could even put two sentences down on paper, he heard the back door open.

Ant rushed to the kitchen to find Roland standing by the door, his tie loose around his neck. The white collared shirt he wore was unbuttoned low enough to show the V-neck T-shirt underneath. He looked . . . weary. Ant watched him take a deep breath, then plaster the biggest smile ever onto his face.

"Hey, baby. Hey, Ant. How was school?"

"Ant had a good day," his mother said, before Ant could speak up. "How was *your* day?"

"I've had better."

Yolanda Joplin leaned in, like she was hoping for more. But Ant's father—suddenly stiff and tight-lipped—had nothing to offer.

"Mrs. Isley called," his mother continued. "She said that you didn't come into the office today."

He placed his briefcase down by the door. It tilted, then fell over. "If you must know, I had some errands to run."

"She tried to call but couldn't reach you," she said. "Maybe something's wrong with your phone?"

Roland glanced at Ant. "Mind handing your momma some worms, son? For all that fishing she's doing?"

Yolanda straightened up. "Roland, that's not fair. I'm just—"

"I know you're worried," he said. "But really, I'm fine. Things are fine." He tapped Ant on the top of the head as he walked toward the hallway. "I just want to lie down for a second. Get off my feet. Rest my eyelids." He paused. "And later on, I want to hear how school went, okay, Ant?"

Ant nodded, but Roland was too busy walking away to notice.

# CHAPTER 16

After all the hoopla, Ant's mother wasn't so keen on cooking, so instead she told Ant to call the pizza place.

He ordered her favorite toppings—pepperoni and mushroom—but she didn't even look in the box. She was quieter than Ant could ever remember, alternating between fidgeting on the sofa and pacing the length of the living room. Ant ended up eating at the kitchen table with only his writing notebook for company.

Before his mom disappeared into her bedroom for the evening, she told Ant that for the time being, they should keep the "incident" at school between them. She planned to tell Ant's father, but only when the time was right.

Ant wasn't about to argue, especially if it meant that he wasn't in trouble.

Later that night, he called his brother. Usually, Yolanda took Ant's phone away before going to bed so he wouldn't be up all night playing spades online. But just like everything else happening over the past two days, nothing was going the way it usually did.

"Ant!" Aaron yelled into the phone. There was a lot of noise on the other end of the line—loud music and raised voices. "Sorry we didn't get to text more yesterday. How was school?"

"Um, fine," he said. "Is now a good time to talk? You sound busy."

"I always have time for my baby brother," he said. "What's up?"

*I'm not a baby,* Ant wanted to say. But instead, he got to the point of his call. "Today was a strange day. It started with a fight—"

"You were in a fight?!" Aaron yelled.

"Not me." He started from the beginning, rushing through the details before Aaron could ask any questions. "But that's not important." Ant looked around, like he was about to spill a juicy secret. "Something's going on with Dad. He had a big pitch yesterday, but it didn't go well."

"Hmm. The Monroe and Sons account."

Now, Lonnie Monroe was a local legend. He was born

and raised right here in Oak Grove, just like Roland and Yolanda. Was even friends with their saintly parents. He grew from a big-headed, snot-nosed kid to the owner of six dry cleaning stores in the city. Some people even wanted Monroe to run for mayor. But Lonnie always declined—said there wasn't enough money in politics.

And who did he trust with his money? Roland Joplin, that's who. Lonnie was one of Roland's first and best clients. That was Lonnie for you—he always remembered the neighborhood. Never forgot where he came from.

But then old Lonnie messed around and got sick, and his kids took over the business. And, well, some kids—no matter how old they are—have a bad habit of thinking they know better than their elders.

"Ma says that Jerry Monroe's been slowly moving their business to bigger—as in *white*—companies," Aaron said. "Guess they finally did the same with their accounting."

"But Dad has other clients, right?"

"Yeah. But the Monroe and Sons account was really big. And a lot of his smaller clients have been leaving as well. With all the online software available, it's a lot easier to do your own taxes these days." Aaron huffed. "I hope the IRS audits them all."

Ant chewed on that fact for a moment. What did it mean for them? Were they poor now?

"I already know what's going on in that head of yours. Stop worrying. Everything's gonna be fine. Ma's got a good job, and Dad'll bounce back, good as new."

"Okay, but Dad was acting weird. So was Ma."

The music in the background was getting louder. "Hold on," said Aaron. "Let me step outside."

"Are you at a party?"

"My roommate is having a little, uh, get-together," Aaron said. "What can I say—they love having people around."

"Ugh. Sorry."

"No, it's nice," Aaron said. "It's mostly just a bunch of my classmates talking about *Star Trek* and playing music from *Lord of the Rings*." He laughed. "Who would have thought that the flute player would be out-geeked?"

In addition to being great at spades, Aaron also played a mean jazz flute. But some of the guys around the neighborhood wouldn't stop messing with him about it. His brother never seemed to be bothered by it, but Ant couldn't help wondering if Aaron was just putting on his poker face.

"Okay, I'm back," Aaron said after a moment. "Now, what's going on with Dad?"

"He was just . . . *strange*. Him and Ma were fighting. I mean, they weren't arguing exactly. They were fighting with everything that they *weren't* saying."

"Was he drinking?" Aaron asked, his voice louder. More urgent. "Was he drunk?"

"No," Ant said. But then he had to reconsider. He'd never seen his father drink before. Would he even recognize if he was *drunk*?

"I mean, I don't *think* he was drunk—"

"You gotta be sure, Ant."

Ant thought about his cousin Jasper, who always had a little too much to drink at family reunions and cookouts. A few too many would get Jasper bragging about his new car or arguing about politics. And when his wife tried to hush him up, he'd only tell her to mind her business and fix him another drink.

And then there was Mr. Gramm, also known as the unofficial "mayor" of Oak Grove. Rain or shine, he could always be found wearing a pair of beige slacks, a way-too-small undershirt, and a porkpie hat, rocking away in his chair on his porch. Morning, noon, or night, he always carried a red plastic cup full of his special, self-named "Boom Boom" sauce and was ever on the ready to pontificate about anything to *anyone* who was foolish enough to listen.

Nope. Ant's father was *definitely* not acting like that.

"I'm positive," Ant said. "He wasn't drunk."

"Good," Aaron said. "But let me know if things get worse."

"Aaron, what's going on?"

Aaron laughed, but it sounded hollow. "I don't want you to worry about it, little man."

Ant ground his teeth. "Don't call me that," he said. "I'm not little."

"I wasn't taking about size. I was talking about age."

"I'm six years younger than you, not sixty."

"Okay, my bad, *big* man," Aaron said, in that way that signaled he totally meant the opposite of what he was saying. "It's just . . . look, I don't want to put any pressure on you. You're still a kid—and that's okay."

"In other words, I'm not tough enough under pressure."

"I didn't say you—"

"I know Dad used to drink. Then he left to go to a treatment center. So what?" Ant didn't care that he was raising his voice. "At least he got help."

Aaron took a long, deep breath. "It's more complicated than that. But don't sweat it. I'll call Dad tonight. Give him a pep talk. Get him to start thinking straight."

"But I can help."

"You need to let me handle this, baby bro. I don't want—"

Ant was so angry, *he* couldn't think straight, and hung up. Then he stared at the phone, waiting to see if his brother would call back.

When it became clear that *that* wasn't going to happen, Ant sucked up his pride and dialed his brother again.

The phone went straight to voice mail.

Twice in a row.

So much for Aaron always having time for his brother.

# CHAPTER 17

Ant's eyes blinked open as he heard the familiar rumble of his mother's SUV pulling out of the driveway. Sunrise was still hours away, and youngblood had just been in the middle of a fantabulous dream about a certain brown-skinned girl from Texas. He squeezed his eyes shut, hoping—praying—to fall back asleep, but that wasn't in the cards. So he got up to get a glass of milk, thinking that maybe that would help him drift back off to la-la land.

But when he opened his door, a clicking and clacking noise drew him down the hallway toward Aaron's bedroom. As he got closer, he realized that the sounds were the punching of computer keys.

He pushed open the door to find his father sitting on the edge of his brother's twin bed with his laptop perched on his knees, the blue screen illuminating his face.

"Ah, you can't beat this!" his father said to the screen. "A flush trumps your straight any day, playboy. Now pay the piper and—"

"Hey, Dad."

Ant's daddy jumped so high, you'd have thought his name was Jesse Owens. "Boy, you just about gave me a heart attack!"

"Sorry." Ant stepped into the room. "I was just gonna get something to drink."

"Well, hurry up so you can get back to bed." Roland's eyes darted to the screen.

Ant watched his father tap at the keyboard and curse at the screen for a long moment.

"What are you playing?" he asked. Of course, Ant already knew the answer. He may not have been a poker player, but he still knew what a flush and a straight were.

"Alright. If you ain't sleeping, you might as well learn something," his father said, not taking his eyes off the screen. "Look at this hand and tell me what you see."

Ant pushed an empty bag of chips out of the way and sat down on the bed. His father had a two of clubs and two of spades. The flop—the cards on the table that all the players shared—included two jacks. "You've got at least two pair."

"Yeah, but the twos aren't very strong. Which is exactly why I'm doing *this*." His father clicked FOLD. "As I've always said, you've got to know when to hold them . . ."

He looked at Ant, waiting for him to chime in.

"And you've got to know when to fold them?" Ant said, but more like a question than a song.

"Exactly! And if there's anything I know, it's how to play cards." He reached down to pick up a glass of soda from the floor. The ice had almost melted down, leaving watered-down Coke. "I even won three hundred bucks. Pretty good chunk of change, right?"

As Ant saw the familiar smile creeping up onto his father's face, he knew what he was supposed to say. He knew what his dad wanted to hear.

But something was gnawing at him, deep down in the pit of his stomach. This whole situation didn't feel right. "But . . . I thought you said gambling was wrong."

"Yeah, when you're a kid. But it's fine for us adults."

Ant couldn't let it go. "So it's not illegal?"

"Son, *speeding* is illegal, but we still do it when we got someplace important to be." His father took a long sip from his glass, leaving nothing but a single sliver of ice.

"Look, the police have a lot more to worry about than somebody like me playing a little poker. This ain't even a lot of money."

Ant found it interesting that his daddy's big score was now considered nothing but pocket change.

"Shoot, even your granddaddy used to gamble," Roland said.

"But I thought Grandma said that she made him quit."

"Sure, sure . . . *after* he saved enough money to buy their first house." His father nudged Ant. "I'm just playing a little to blow off some steam. I needed it, after how the last two days have gone."

Ant nodded. That *kinda* made sense to him. He liked to play spades and computer games when he was stressed—or when he didn't want to do his homework. Plus, his granddad had been right proud of that house of his.

"And hey," his father said, elbowing him again, "since I'm such a generous guy, maybe I'll give you the honor of grabbing me another bag of chips."

Ant allowed himself to laugh. "If anything, you should be paying me off so I don't tell Ma how you've been eating in Aaron's room. I just hope you didn't spill any crumbs on the bed." Ant started toward the door. "Want me to grab you another soda, too? Are they in the pantry?"

"Um . . ." His father closed the laptop lid. "You know . . . maybe you shouldn't say anything to your mom about this." He motioned to the computer. "*Any* of this."

Ant froze in place, not knowing what to say.

"Think about it like this," his dad continued. "We gamble on things every day. We drive to work—gambling that we won't get into an accident. And we invest in stocks and retirement funds, hoping that they make a profit. Some plans—and people—are very risk-adverse, like your mother. Me? I'm okay with a calculated risk."

"So playing poker is like investing in the stock market?"

Roland nodded. "Now you got it!"

"But Mom'll be mad if the risk doesn't pay off, right?"

His father's eyebrows bunched up, and the smile disappeared from his face.

Ant realized that he'd said the wrong thing. "Never mind," he said, edging away. "I should go back to—"

"No, Anthony. Wait up a minute," his father interrupted. "You're a big kid. Tough. So I'm not gonna to lie to you—your momma is worried." He took a deep breath. "You know I used to have—I mean, back when you were a little kid . . ." He paused to take another breath. "I guess what I'm trying to say is—back in the day, I was a bit too free-spirited with the hooch."

Ant turned away from his father. It felt off to be looking at him right then. He wasn't used to his daddy being so vulnerable. "Yeah, but that was a long time ago," Ant said. "And you went to those AA meetings and you were away at that—"

"Whoa, there," his father said. "Just to be clear, I wasn't an alcoholic. Not a real one."

"You didn't go to one of those six-week rehabilitation clinics?"

Roland shook his head. "Those places are for real drunks."

"But I thought . . ." Ant didn't know how to ask the question on his mind. Or even if he really understood what he wanted to know. "Where did you go when—"

"It wasn't like I was stumbling around, dressed like a hobo, stinkin' up the place. I wasn't like Mr. Gramm on his porch with that red plastic cup of his. I just got a little carried away. You know, too many late nights with the guys. It was a way to deal with stress. That sort of thing. But when I finally shook the habit, I promised your momma that I would never take another drink." He placed one hand over his heart and raised the other like he was taking an oath. "I swear, I've never been bad at gambling,

Ant. Just at gambling and drinking at the same time. So as long as I don't drink . . ."

"Then you can gamble?"

He nodded. "I want you and your brother to have all the things that I wasn't able to have when I was a kid. I want you to go to the best schools, have the best education." His father bent to pick up his glass, before realizing that it was empty. "And I want your momma to have good things, too."

"I know, Dad."

"Good. Then we're on the same page." He held up his hand for a high five. "Can I count on you?"

Ant looked at his dad's open palm. "You mean, not to mention this to Ma?"

"I'm not going to do this forever. Just long enough for business to pick up." Then, apparently, Roland got tired of holding his hand up, so he plopped it down on top of his laptop. "I've already got some new clients lined up. But you know folks and their money. It takes them a while to cut that check." He looked Ant right in the eyes. "I need you to be my partner, Anthony. I need you to back me up. Okay, little man?"

Ant still didn't appreciate being called "little." But as he nodded back at his father, he realized that it didn't sound so bad when it came from his dad.

# CHAPTER 18

Later that morning, Ant left for school much earlier than usual. The weather seemed to match his foul mood. A storm was brewing, and it was so overcast that my man couldn't even see his shadow. Not that he was paying attention to the sky or even the sidewalk. He had too many other things on this mind.

For one, he was nervous about keeping his father's gambling a secret. He was scared about what would happen if his mother found out. And he was worried about Jamal, and what would happen if he wasn't able to play in the tournament.

But more than anything, he was thinking about his daddy's history with drinking.

His brother had turned so serious when he'd brought it

up the night before. Meanwhile, his father had been so . . . *flippant.* Like it wasn't something anyone should be worried about.

Aaron had been adamant about knowing whether their dad was at it again. "You gotta be sure," he'd told Ant. But how was Ant supposed to do that? Honestly, he didn't even know what alcohol smelled like, aside from that horrible clear stuff his momma was always rubbing on him to get him extra clean. And Ant was pretty sure that rubbing alcohol was way different than the type you drank.

That's why Ant left the house early. He needed to see what *drunk* looked like for himself.

When he got to Magnolia Street, he took a little detour from his usual route to school. And sure enough, a half block later, he spotted Shadrach Gramm sitting in a rocking chair on his front porch, a red plastic cup already in hand.

Some people said that Mr. Gramm was in his eighties, but no one really knew for sure. With his shrunken frame and droopy eyes, he kinda looked like a skeleton wearing a cloak of wrinkled, moly brown skin. But those skinny fingers had a tight grip around his cup, that's for sure.

"Hey, Little Joplin," Mr. Gramm called from the porch. "Ain't you got school today?"

"Yes, sir," Ant answered, his legs powering him forward. "I'm heading there now. I just decided to take the long way."

"Good. Y'all young'uns need to get as much exercise as you can, instead of spending all day inside, fiddling around on the internet and everything. You know all those infrared beams from those computers and phones scramble your brain."

"Shad, will you shut up and leave that boy alone?" Ms. Frances poked her head out of the door. "Hey, Anthony. How's everybody at home? And how's your brother?" She waved him up the porch steps.

Ant slowed down. It was one thing to sprint past Mr. Gramm. But he couldn't do that to Mr. Gramm's sister. His momma had raised him to respect his elders. To listen when he was being spoken to. Plus, Ms. Frances was a church lady. She was there all the time—Tuesday, Wednesday, and twice on Sundays. You don't ignore a lady who does that much talking to God. Trust me—it's just asking for trouble.

Ant climbed the two steps but didn't go any farther. The musty smell of sweat and the sharpness of whatever was in Mr. Gramm's cup lingered around the porch like a fog. Up close, he could see the man's bloodshot, unfocused eyes looking right through him. Every time Mr. Gramm exhaled, he pushed stale, heavy breath into Ant's face.

"Everyone at home is good," he told Ms. Frances, even though he wasn't quite sure if that was correct or not. "Aaron started school this week, too."

"Well, tell your momma that I'm praying for him," said Ms. Frances. "And we've got a special youth service going on this Wednesday if you—"

"You think that boy wants to go to church on a Wednesday? He's probably bored enough going on Sundays." Mr. Gramm took a sip from his cup and winced. "But since you're standing there, Joplin, why don't you run over to Eugene's place and pick me up a pack of MoonPies and a bottle of grapefruit juice? I don't have my wallet on me, but tell him I'm good for it."

"He will do no much thing. Didn't you hear the boy say that he was on his way to school?" Ms. Frances put her hands on her hips. "I'm sure you can manage drinking your vodka without grapefruit juice for a day." She shook her head. "I'm just glad Mama died before she could see how you turned out."

"What? I'm retired. Can't I drink when I want to?"

"Shad, getting fired ain't the same as retirement."

"When it happened over thirty years ago, it's called retirement."

Ant had seen enough. "I'll see y'all later," he called as he headed down the steps. Ms. Frances waved goodbye to him, while Mr. Gramm took another sip from his cup.

Ant's entire body relaxed as he headed down the block. As unpleasant as that encounter had been, it had made him feel a whole lot better. 'Cause if *that* was what a drunk was like, he didn't have a thing to worry about. His daddy was just fine.

# CHAPTER 19

Youngblood's attitude may have improved after his little detour, but the weather sure didn't. Just as Ant turned the corner, it started pouring. Hard. He pulled out his umbrella, but he was still soaked by the time he got to school.

Worse, since he was early, he had to report to the gymnasium, where he'd have to sit quietly in a line and read until the morning bell. Why had he left his house so early again?

The air inside the gym was heavy and humid. Ant walked to the back of the line and dropped to the floor. Then a younger boy with an umbrella almost bigger than he was fell in behind Ant.

*Great,* Ant thought. *I'm not even lucky enough to sit by my friends.*

But sometimes lady luck shines on you when you least expect it. Moments later, Jamal busted through the gym doors. Ant hadn't expected to see his friend for who knew how long—not if he'd been suspended.

Ant glanced at the kid beside him, who was struggling to secure the tie around his umbrella. "Mind switching places?" Ant asked. "My friend's coming."

The kid shook his head. "I don't think we're supposed to do that."

Ant took the kid's umbrella and snapped it closed. "The teachers won't even notice."

"Thanks," the kid said, taking the umbrella back. "But I don't think so."

Ant looked over at the teachers. Mr. Hoyt and Coach Hughey were too busy talking to be paying attention to them. "What's your name?" he asked the boy. "How old are you?"

"Bobby. I'm in second grade."

Ant thought about how his dad or Aaron would handle it. "We're not switching places, really. It's more like—I'm getting out of line, and then you're moving up, and then I'm getting back in line behind you. It's like I'm going to the bathroom, then coming back."

"You're going to the bathroom?"

"No." Ant sighed. "I'd be *pretending* to go to the— Just switch with me, okay?"

Clearly, youngblood still has a lot to learn about smooth-talking kids.

By this time, Jamal had trudged into line behind the four-footer. He gave Ant a head nod but didn't say anything.

"Come on," Ant said. "Please?"

Bobby looked up at the ceiling and stroked his chin. "How much you got on you?"

"What?"

"Money? Pay me and I'll switch."

"I'm not . . ." Ant huffed. "Fine. How about fifty cents?"

"Make it a dollar, and we got a deal." The kid grinned like he'd stolen something—'cause really, he kinda had—and stuck his hand out while Ant opened his wallet.

Ant passed him the money, and Bobby smugly hopped in front of him.

"Dude, what happened?" Ant whispered once he was finally sitting beside Jamal.

Jamal shook his head. "Don't want to talk. Don't want to get in trouble."

"No way! I spent a whole dollar just so I could get the scoop. I heard you got suspended."

Jamal lowered his head, trying to hide his mouth. "No. Dr. Knight sent us home for the day, and put us in ISS for the rest of the week."

In-school suspension. That was way better than the alternative. "How mad was your aunt when she found out?" Ant had considered name-dropping Jamal's mom so his friend wouldn't realize Ant already knew she wasn't around. But Ant was tired of playing games, of always having to pretend that he didn't know what was going on.

"On a scale of one to ten?" Jamal sighed. "Twenty."

"So I guess that means you can't play in the tournament next weekend."

"Man, I'll be lucky if I'm still *alive* next weekend. Rebbie was fuming! I explained how it wasn't my fault—"

"But . . . it kinda was."

Jamal frowned. "RJ was talking about my momma. What was I supposed to do?"

"You know RJ. He's always talking trash."

"He crossed a line, Ant."

"Do I hear talking down there?" a stern voice called.

Ant turned to see Mr. Hoyt glaring at them. "Didn't y'all learn your lesson yesterday?"

"Sorry," they mumbled.

Mr. Hoyt gave them an extra-long, extra-intense *"Don't*

*make me have to say it again"* stare, then returned to his conversation with Coach Hughey.

Ant sat there, lips zipped. *What am I supposed to do about the tournament now?* he wondered.

But when he glanced back at his best friend, he remembered that some things were more important than spades.

"I'm really sorry about your mom," Ant whispered. "When did she leave? While you were with your dad?"

"You heard, huh?" Jamal kept his head bowed. "I guess everyone in Oak Grove knows."

"We don't have to talk about it. I just—"

"Naw, it's cool," Jamal said. "Yeah, she took off last month, while I was in Philly. She says she's looking for a job in Atlanta and will be back soon, but I've heard that before."

This was the third, fourth, or maybe even fifth time that Jamal's mom had bailed on him and his brother. What can I say—a soggy paper towel was more dependable than Loretta Williams. Still, that didn't stop Jamal from hoping each time would be different.

"Sorry about the tournament," Jamal said. "I know how badly you want to play in it."

Ant didn't say anything. It hadn't dawned on him that

not playing was an option. That Jamal might expect him to miss the tournament completely.

"Ant?" Jamal nudged him. "We good? I promise, I'll make it up to you."

"Yeah, we're good," Ant mumbled. He couldn't look Jamal in the eye as they bumped fists. "But no more secrets, okay?"

Jamal nodded. "Deal."

# CHAPTER 20

Now, Ant felt sorry for Jamal and all—really, he did. Jamal's mom leaving was a bum deal. So was in-school suspension.

But Ant wasn't keen on sitting out of the tournament just because Jamal decided to up and clobber another kid at school. Not when his father expected him to play—and to win. But how was he supposed to be loyal to his best friend and make his father happy at the same time?

Of course, Ant didn't know if he could even find another partner before the tournament. He thought about asking Cordell. If RJ's parents had barred him from playing, maybe Cordell would be looking for a new partner, too. But when Ant asked him about it on the way to class, he discovered that he and RJ were both still in. Dwayne's mother didn't let him play games where people could win real money—never mind all those dollar scratch-offs she bought at the Quick Mart every week. And Terrence, bless his heart, would never learn to play well enough in time.

Honestly, there was really only one person good enough for Ant to partner with.

One *girl*.

But he didn't see how he could ask Shirley without upsetting Jamal.

Plus, who knew if Shirley even wanted to play? Sure, they'd gotten along okay over the past couple of days. But working with a spades partner wasn't just about being able to hold a conversation. It was about anticipating what your partner was about to say—about to *do*—in any situation. It was a bond that took months, if not years, to form. And it wasn't something you did just because you *thought* you *might* have a little crush on someone.

Ant was still stewing over this as Mr. Reese walked to the middle of the room. "Good morning! Since y'all like competitions so much, I want you all to work on this puzzle in your groups."

Almost everyone's hand popped up.

"And before you ask, there's no prize." Mr. Reese flipped on the projector. "Good luck."

Ant leaned in as the words of the puzzle appeared on the screen.

**Read the sentence below. Whichever team comes up with the correct answers—and an explanation for how you arrived at them—will win.**

***Ethan and Elle walked through a muddy riverbed.***

**How many *E*s are in this sentence?**

"That's easy." Layla crossed her arms. "It's six, right? Three in their names, one in *walked,* and two in *riverbed.*"

Rochelle nodded, as did Terrence. "Should we tell Mr. Reese?" Terrence asked, his arm already creeping up. "I don't want another team to answer before us."

"Why?" Rochelle added. "It's not like we win anything."

Shirley and Ant remained silent, as they read, reread, and then reread *again* the words on the screen.

"Uh . . . hello?" Layla said to Shirley and Ant. "Y'all there?"

Across the room, Yvonne's hand shot into the air.

"Shoot!" Terrence said. "I wanted us to be first."

Shirley turned back to the group. "What if it's asking for the number of *E*s in the *last* sentence?"

Ant was impressed. He hadn't thought of that.

"Read it again," Shirley continued. "Mr. Reese asked for the *E*s in *this* sentence."

Layla frowned. "But that's a question, not a sentence."

"A question *is* a sentence," Ant and Shirley said at the same time. Then they looked at each other and smiled.

"So if it's the last sentence . . . question . . . whatever, then is the answer five?" Rochelle asked.

Meanwhile, across the room, Yvonne whispered her cluster's answer to Mr. Reese. He shook his head. "Incorrect," he said. "But good try, Badgers."

"Wait . . . which answer is correct?" Terrence asked. "Five or six?"

"It's both," Ant said. "Look—he's asked for the correct answer*s*."

"Oh—it's plural!" Shirley said. "But wait . . . maybe the question only asked for the number of *E*s in the phrase 'this sentence.'

"But see how *E* is capitalized?" Ant pointed at the screen. "Maybe that means he's only looking for capital *E*s. Or just *E* sounds?" Ant said.

"Like the *y* in *muddy*?" Shirley replied.

"Yeah!"

For the next five minutes, Terrence, Layla, and Rochelle sat and watched as Ant and Shirley tossed ideas back and forth like a tennis ball bouncing across a net. Soon they were even completing each other's sentences.

When it was all said and done, the Dolphins had won with ten unique answer and rationalization combos.

Mr. Reese nodded at them. "Good job, Dolphins. I don't think I've ever gotten that many possible answers."

Rochelle snorted as Mr. Reese walked off. "You mean, good job, Ant and Shirley," she whispered.

"Y'all are really smart," Layla added. "I'm glad we're in y'all's group."

Ant felt the same way. Or at least he did about Shirley being in the group. She was quick. They thought alike and laughed at the same things. She'd make a great partner for the tournament.

But would she want to play with him?

# CHAPTER 21

After school, Ant was surprised to see Jamal hanging around outside, texting someone, his thumbs flying faster than Ant had ever seen them.

"You waiting on me?" Ant asked as he approached. "I figured Rebbie would have you sprinting home like you're Usain Bolt."

"Funny," Jamal said. "But no lie—she straight-up told me no lollygagging after school."

"*Lollygagging*? When did Rebbie start talking like old people?"

"She's thirty-five, Ant. She's been old for a long time."

Ant's eyes widened. "Ooooh . . . you'd better be glad we're friends. If we weren't, I'd tell Rebbie. I'm surprised she didn't take your cell phone away."

"Oh, she did. I'm only allowed to carry it to and from school." He pocketed the phone. "Hey . . . walk with me on the way home, okay?"

"Um . . . sure."

Ant fell into step beside Jamal. He remained quiet as Jamal went on and on about how boring ISS was. But soon, the conversation turned to what Jamal had missed in class that day . . . and Shirley. Ant told Jamal about the group puzzle—but didn't mention how well he and Shirley had worked together.

"That dumb girl ain't giving you a hard time anymore, is she?"

"No, we're good," Ant said. "And trust me, she's not dumb. Not by a long shot."

In fact, I'd wager that Shirley was as far from dumb as the moon is from Mars. And young Ant had most definitely taken notice. He still wasn't convinced that he was ready to be swapping spit or anything like that. But he mighta been starting to think that holding hands wouldn't be so bad after all.

Jamal clearly thought otherwise. "I don't know, man. She's . . . too much."

Ant shook his head. But there was no point in arguing. He knew it would take a lot more than one conversation for Jamal to change his mind about Shirley.

A few minutes later, they reached Jamal's house. "I guess I'd better get out of here," Ant said. He was pretty sure Rebbie wouldn't appreciate Ant and Jamal hanging out while he was on punishment.

"Actually, could you hold up a second? Taj, um, wanted to holla at you real quick. That's who I was texting at school."

Sure enough, Jamal's brother chose right then to step outside. He must have been on the way to work—he wore his Oil Zone collared shirt and a cocky smirk.

"Wassup, Ant," Taj said as he walked toward them. "What you been up to?"

"Nothing much," Ant said as they dapped.

"You mean nothing, other than falling in *love* with the new girl at school," Jamal said.

"Is that right?" Taj stroked his chin. "At least one of you is man enough to step to a girl. I keep telling Jamal that people are gonna start looking at him funny if he don't start talking to females soon."

There were so, so, so many things that Ant wanted to say, but he figured that maybe it would just be best to extract himself from the situation. Taj was the last person he wanted to get love advice from.

Not that he was in love, mind you. No siree.

"I don't even like her like that," Ant said. "But listen, I'll catch y'all later."

"Don't be mad and walk off because we're talking about your girlfriend," Taj said. "We'll chill out, little man."

Ant sighed. "She's *not* my girlfriend."

"You know the more you say you don't like her, the more it sounds like you do," Jamal said.

"Which, again, is cool," Taj added. "You ain't got to apologize for liking a girl. Just don't be a wuss about it. Not like your brother."

"My brother's not a wuss!"

Taj held up his hands. "Calm down. I don't mean no disrespect, but let's keep it real—your brother is a total poindexter when it comes to girls. Always trying to be polite. Always afraid to make a move." Taj popped his knuckles. "That fool got friend-zoned by super-fine Nia Ingram. Ain't that something?"

"But they *were* just friends."

"No sixteen-year-old guy wants to be *just* friends with a girl," Taj said. "They get stuck there because they don't know how to step to females. 'Cause they're too afraid to take charge." Taj walked over and draped his arm around

Ant's neck, his elbow heavy on Ant's shoulder. "In the game of love, there are those who conquer, and those who *are* conquered. You ain't no gazelle. You're a lion, my man. A lion."

*Please don't make me roar* was all Ant could think.

"Here's what I want you to do. Tomorrow, I want you to holla at the girl. Give her a compliment. But nothing too fancy. And say it all nonchalant . . . like you don't care. You don't want to look weak." He thumped Ant on the chest. "This ain't checkers. It's chess. You're the king hunting your queen."

Ant was pretty sure that the *queen* was the most powerful piece on a chessboard, not the king. The king seemed to do more hiding than hunting. But Ant didn't consider Taj the type to get hung up on details.

"I'll keep all that in mind," Ant said. "I'd better get home."

He started to pull away, but Taj tightened his armlock on him. "Hey, before you go, let me talk to you about one more thing." Taj flexed his bicep, pressing it against Ant's neck. "The next time my brother gets into a fight, I'ma need you to have his back."

"Taj . . ." Jamal started.

"No, he needs to hear this," Taj said. "Look, you and

my brother have been tight since y'all were babies. He's your best friend, right?"

Ant nodded. "Yeah."

"So when he gets jumped, you're supposed to get in there with him. You wouldn't let your brother scrap alone, would you?"

"No, I guess not," Ant mumbled. But then again, he had never seen his brother come close to getting in a fight.

"Alright, that's what I want to hear." Taj let go of him, and Ant had to stop himself from rubbing his neck. "I don't care how small you are," Taj said. "Don't ever be weak. Be a lion."

# CHAPTER 22

Ant spent the rest of the walk home fuming about what Taj had said. But if Ant was being right honest with himself, he was just as mad at Jamal as he was at Taj. Jamal hadn't called Ant *weak,* but he also hadn't done anything to defend him in front of his brother.

He thought about calling Aaron to talk about it, but Ant still wasn't ready to forgive him for all those "little" comments.

Then he saw his mother's SUV in the carport, and pushed aside everything he'd just been stewing about. Just like yesterday, she was home early. Did that mean something had happened with his dad?

When he opened the back door, he expected to see his mother pacing the kitchen. Instead, he was greeted with the smooth sounds of old-school soul music floating through the air, along with the smell of burnt chicken.

"Thank goodness you're here," his mother said, stepping into view from around the corner. "Drop your backpack and give me a hand, sweetie."

"Sure thing. But aren't you supposed to be at work?"

"I decided to take off early again. Your daddy's had a rough few days, so I wanted to treat him to a special dinner just like your grandma used to make on Sundays after church." Yolanda waved away the smoke from her burnt chicken. "But I couldn't remember if I was supposed to cook the chicken at three hundred and fifty degrees or four hundred and fifty degrees."

Ant glanced at the chicken. "I'm pretty sure it was supposed to be three hundred and fifty."

"Yeah, I figured that out." His mother winked. "But no sweat. Your momma's always prepared. I bought two chickens. And we've got to hurry if we want to have dinner ready by the time your dad comes home. I still have to cook the cabbage and rice. I was thinking about making a cobbler, too, though I don't think we'll have time."

Cabbage? Rice? Peach cobbler? His mother never cooked like this. Not even during the holidays.

Ant watched his mother dump the whole chicken

into the garbage. It was still smoking. "Um, maybe we should call Grandma," Ant suggested. "I bet she'd be happy to give us some pointers." His grandmother lived in an assisted-living facility near her sister in Columbia. Roland had offered to let his mother live with them, but she declined. The food was better at Century Gardens.

"There are some things that I can do without your grandmother's help, thank you very much." She sighed. "Now put your stuff down and help me finish dinner."

Ant dropped his backpack off in his room, then returned to the kitchen. The new chicken sat on the counter, along with each and every spice jar from the cupboard.

"Ma, are you sure all those spices go together?" Ant asked.

"I guess we'll find out soon enough." She chuckled. "I hope your father appreciates all the hassle I'm going through. It'd be a lot easier to order out."

"Then why don't we?"

His mother kept her focus on the chicken, sprinkling pepper on it, over and over and over.

"Ma?" Ant took a step forward. "Do we not have the money?"

"We're okay!" Mercifully, she stopped seasoning the

chicken. "I mean, we will be. You know your father lost a few accounts?"

Ant nodded. "I know."

"Your daddy's been pounding the pavement, trying to drum up more business. But it's hard. Tax season is half a year away. Even if he signs a new client, we won't see anything right away. And private school ain't cheap."

"Will Aaron have to come back home?" He'd gotten a small scholarship to attend Mitchell, but their parents still had to foot most of the bill.

"No. Absolutely not," she said. "Your father would never forgive himself if . . . You know what, forget I said anything about it." She looked down at the chicken. "Whew, that's a lot of pepper. Come help me rinse this thing off."

Ant turned on the water and helped her wash off the chicken. He wondered if his mother would feel better knowing that his dad was making some money online. But part of "having his dad's back" meant that Ant had to keep that secret to himself, no matter how much it made his stomach churn.

"Earth to Anthony," his mother said. "What's going on in that head of yours?"

Ant blinked, then looked down at the chicken. "Just thinking about Dad."

"Oh, honey. Don't worry. Everything's going to be fine." His mother put the chicken in the pan again. While her back was turned, her voice seemed to shrink. "Not that I want you spying on your father, but you'll let me know if anything seems . . . off, right?"

Ant froze.

She turned around toward him. "Ant?"

"Um . . . sure." He hesitated. "But what do you mean by *off*?"

"You're a smart boy. You'll know when something feels wrong."

Ant knew, alright. But it was one thing to feel it, and a whole 'nother thing to speak up about it.

"Let's change the subject," his mom said. "Are you and Jamal ready for the tournament?"

"Actually, Jamal can't play. Because of the fight. So I've been thinking about asking . . . a friend to be my partner. But do you think it's disloyal to play with someone else?"

"Your grandfather used to say, 'Loyalty does not trump stupidity.' In other words—you don't have to give up what you want just because someone else made a boneheaded mistake." She caught Ant's eye and held it. "But you should probably be honest with Jamal about it."

*Ugh*. Ant didn't know what worried him more—confronting Jamal or convincing Shirley to be his partner.

"So who are you thinking about asking?"

"Oh, no one special," Ant said as he began fiddling with his fingernails. "Just a new girl from school."

"That's nice, honey." Yolanda returned to the sink to wash her hands. "And does this girl have a name?"

"Um, Shirley Heyward. She just moved here."

"Oh! That's Joanie Mae's kid! I heard that she and her family had moved back into her parents' old house." She nodded at Ant, then at the still-running faucet. "Your turn. The last thing I need is everyone getting salmonella up in here."

Ant squirted a blob of liquid soap onto his hands, sudsed them up good, then ran them through the water.

"For longer than five seconds, please."

Ant stuck his hands back underneath the faucet. "I made up for the lack of water with extra soap."

"Yeah, right," she said. "Well, I'm sure you and Shirley will do great in the tournament. I'm looking forward to rooting you on." She grabbed the salt in one hand and pepper in the other. "Not that it's about winning or losing. Just try your best."

Ant turned off the water. He hated it when his mother

said things like that. He knew that she was trying to be supportive—but to Ant, it felt like she was saying, *It's okay that you crack under pressure. At least you're trying.* He never remembered her saying stuff like that to Aaron, about cards or anything else. But of course, Aaron had never run off after losing a game.

"It's got to be hard, starting a new school and everything," she said as she moved on to a spice that Ant didn't even know how to pronounce. "Maybe Shirley will make a few more friends at the tournament."

"Ma, a spades tournament ain't—*isn't*—really the place to get all friendly with the competition. That's like giving a compliment to a cow before you turn it into a hamburger."

"That sounds like something your grandfather used to say, too." She stopped seasoning and cocked her head at the chicken, as if she wanted it to tell her whether she'd spiced it up enough. "Why does everything have to be such a competition between boys? Your father was the same way."

"Did you and Dad play together when y'all were in high school?"

"Oh, not at all. First, there was no way I could be your dad's spades partner. He talked way too much trash. Plus, back then, a lot of people didn't consider it ladylike to play cards."

Ant chewed on the bottom of his lip, then asked, "But it's okay now, right?"

"Of course it is, sweetie. It was okay back then, too." She opened the oven door. "Let me guess. Are you worried some of the kids will give you a hard time about playing with Shirley?"

"Just a few," Ant said. *Or one.*

"Don't listen to them. They're idiots." She placed the bird in the oven and closed the door with her foot. "*You* don't think it's a big deal to play with a girl, do you?"

Ant vigorously shook his head. "Nope. No way."

"Okay, then it's officially *not* a big deal."

"It's not even a *little* deal."

"Gotcha." His mom double-checked the oven's temperature.

"I'm just thinking about playing with her because she's good," Ant continued. "That's it. I barely notice she's a girl. And who knows—she might not even want to be partners."

"Sure. I understand," his mother said. Her face was as long as a loaf of bread, without the smallest hint of a smile on her lips.

I guess the Joplin men weren't the only ones who knew how to sport a poker face.

# CHAPTER 23

Ant and his mother had all the food on the table by a quarter after five. Yolanda had even called ahead and had gotten Roland to promise to come home right after work, in order to "help Ant get ready for the tournament."

But when the clock rolled around to six thirty and Roland still hadn't shown up, Yolanda told Ant to go ahead and start eating.

"Maybe you should call Dad again," Ant offered.

The look on Yolanda's face let Ant know that that wasn't an option.

As they were finishing the meal—which, on the Yolanda scale, was pretty good—they heard his dad's sedan pull into the driveway. A moment later, his father opened the door, all smiles.

"Hey, guys!" He took a deep breath. "Something smells good. What are we having?"

Ant glanced at his mother. He wasn't sure if he was supposed to answer.

"Hello, Roland," his mother said, her gaze focused on the carved-up bird in front of her, not the door. She sniffed the air and quickly spun toward her husband.

Roland's smile evaporated. "What? I forget an anniversary?"

"No, you didn't." She inhaled deeply, her fists clenching her utensils. "But it would have been considerate of you to come home when you said you would. In fact, I believe I specifically asked you to."

With all the sniffing she was doing, Ant wondered if his mother was trying to tell if his dad had been drinking.

"I'm sorry," Roland said. "But you know how it is . . ."

"Yeah. Sometimes the clients set the hours," she said. "Convenient."

Ant's father sidled over to the table, and Ant could finally smell what his momma must have noticed.

Roland Joplin smelled like smoke.

Although Ant had never seen his father drink alcohol, he knew Roland used to be a smoker. But he'd quit that cold turkey when Ant's granddaddy was diagnosed with lung cancer. After Granddad died, Roland had threatened to wear out both boys' rear ends if he ever caught one of them even thinking about puffing on a cigarette.

"Well, I'm here now! I can't believe you cooked all this." Roland picked up a piece of cabbage from Yolanda's plate. "But I gotta be honest, I kinda wish y'all had told me earlier, since I already ate at—" Roland probably noticed the death rays coming from Yolanda's eyes, because he quickly changed his response. "Then again, who could pass up a feast like this?" He leaned over and pecked Yolanda's cheek. "Why don't you go ahead and fix me a plate. I'll be back in a second."

His father disappeared down the hallway.

His mother remained in her seat.

"You want me to grab a plate for Dad?" Ant offered.

"I'll deal with it," she said. But she kept right on sitting in her chair.

About ten minutes later, Roland emerged from his bedroom whistling the melody to "The Gambler."

He headed to his usual spot—the head of the table—but stopped when he noticed that the place setting was empty. "Where's my plate? In the microwave?"

"In the cabinet, along with the other plates," Yolanda said. "You want to eat, you can fix it yourself."

Roland stopped grinning. "What's wrong? I apologized for being late. The next time you want me home for dinner, just tell me you're cooking."

"It was supposed to be a surprise."

"Well, color me surprised, then."

Ant cleared his throat. "Really, I don't mind fixing—"

"Anthony Arnold Joplin, you better keep your narrow butt right in that chair," his mother snapped.

"You don't have to yell at the boy," Roland said. "Besides, it's not a man's job to fix another man's plate of food."

"That sounds like something Jasper would say," Yolanda mumbled.

His father waved his hand dismissively. "Ah, Jasper ain't so bad."

That made his mother sit up. "I thought y'all weren't on speaking terms."

Ant didn't know his cousin Jasper all that well. They only saw him about three times a year—at cookouts and family get togethers. But from his mother's snide comments, Ant figured that was three times too many.

Ant's father walked to the cabinet. "Water under the bridge. He's giving me a lead on some new clients. Looking out for family—like he's supposed to."

"Hmm. And is he still making all those trips up to North Carolina?" she asked.

Ant's father silently returned to the table, plate in hand. He sat down, then started serving himself big, heaping scoops of cabbage and rice like he was trying to eat for four people.

Ant's mother took another deep breath, seemingly to calm her nerves. She even closed her eyes and pinched her fingers like all the hippies and millennials do when they're meditating. Then she looked at Roland, her face softer.

"Just . . . tell me what's going on, babe." She reached out and took her husband's hand—mahogany brown on pecan tan. "We're a team, remember?"

For a moment, time seemed to stand still. Roland's eyes got all large and his lips parted. He leaned in, and whatever was on his tongue seemed bound to just spill out.

But as quickly as it had come, the moment passed, and Ant wasn't sure why. In a flash, his dad's mouth snapped shut, his eyes went back to normal, and that same old grin popped up on his face.

"Everything's fine, Yolanda. I've got a plan, and I promise, I'll fill you in as soon as I put it in motion. Trust me—I know what I'm doing."

His mother's shoulders drooped. "Okay, Roland."

Ant couldn't help feeling a little mad at his dad. He always wanted to be the head of the family and make all the decisions—about how to run his business or where his sons went to school or what he did with their money—on his own. That wasn't how teams worked. You had to trust your partners, not keep secrets from them. But at least his parents weren't going to fight anymore.

His dad picked up his fork. "Now let's eat! I'm starving! Can't let all this good food go to waste."

His mother nodded, then grabbed a drumstick and dropped it onto her plate.

Ant did the same.

And that's how Ant ate his fourth meal of the day.

# CHAPTER 24

The next morning, Ant woke up before the alarm clock went off. He slowly slipped out of his room and held his breath. Sure enough, he could hear the clicking of a keyboard coming from Aaron's room.

Ant made a big production of storming down the hallway, yanking open the bathroom door, and slamming it shut behind him. When he'd finished, Aaron's door was open and the light was off.

Apparently, his father had gotten the point.

Ant got dressed, all the while thinking about how to ask his dad why he needed to play online poker in secret.

But Ant didn't have a chance to ask a single thing. As soon as he stepped foot in the kitchen, his father started in on him like stink on a dung beetle.

"I hear Jamal's got a mean right hook," his father said.

Ant stopped in his tracks. "Ma told you about the fight?"

"Last night." He paused to take a lengthy sip from his coffee cup. "Took her long enough."

Ant's face fell. "I'm sorry. Ma thought that we shouldn't—"

"Don't worry, we talked it out. She also told me that you weren't involved." He winked. "You know us Joplin men—we're lovers, not fighters."

True enough. Youngblood breathed a sigh of relief. At least that was one less secret he had to keep. Just because the boy *had* a good poker face didn't mean he wanted to use it.

"Jamal's mad because I didn't help him," Ant said.

"What did he expect you to do? It was a one-on-one fight, right?"

Ant nodded. That was true, except Cordell had jumped into the fray to break it up, but Ant hadn't. He wondered if that made him . . . *weak*. "But what if it'd been two on one? Are there times when it's worth fighting?"

"It's complicated, Ant. I promise, we'll talk more tonight." His father rose from the table, grabbing his cup. "You know, I think I'm going to work from home today."

Ant had never known his father to do that before.

Shucks—even when it was sleeting and snowing, his father was always antsy to get out the door.

"Maybe we can even get in some spades practice before dinner." His father held out his hand for a fist bump. "Sound good?"

"Sounds great!"

But just as Ant and his father knocked fists, Ant got a whiff of his father's cup.

Now, it wasn't like the boy was being nosy or looking to catch his father in the act. But young Ant still had his brother's cautionary words running through his brain on a loop.

"What are you drinking?" Ant asked.

His father froze. "Excuse me?" There was an edge to his voice.

"No! I just meant—it doesn't smell like coffee. Trying something new?"

His father relaxed. "It's only grapefruit juice. Bought some the other day. Just had a hankering for it."

Ant did his best to swallow the lump in his throat. *Maybe I'm overthinking things,* he told himself. *A lot of people drink grapefruit juice. So what if I've never seen him drink it before. And who cares that Mr. Gramm drinks the same thing. It doesn't mean anything.*

"You okay, son?"

Ant took a step forward. There was only one way to find out for sure. "Um . . . could I have a taste?"

His father nervously glanced down at his cup, which seemed almost halfway full. Then he tilted his head back and downed the contents in one shot. "Sorry, all out!" He flashed Ant that trademark Joplin grin. "If I remember, I'll pick up some more from the Quick Mart this afternoon."

*Just like Mr. Gramm.* Ant forced himself to smile when it was the absolute last thing he wanted to do. "Okay, Dad."

And as his father walked away, the only thing Ant was left to wonder was if he was going to grab some MoonPies as well.

# CHAPTER 25

Ant was in a deep, dark haze all the way to school.

Shucks, I was, too.

Ant didn't know for sure if his father was drinking, but as those fancy TV lawyers say, the circumstantial evidence was quite compelling. He considered texting his brother just so he'd have *someone* to talk to about it, but then he decided against it. He didn't want Aaron worrying about something that might not even be true. Plus, he already felt crummy. No need for his brother to feel the same way.

Just then Ant spotted Jamal at the corner ahead of him. Once Ant realized that Jamal was waiting for *him,* his demeanor shifted from confusion to anger.

"Looking for me?" Ant barked.

I was actually a little proud of the fella, putting some bass in his voice.

"Look, Ant," Jamal began. "I'm sorry about what my brother said. I know you were trying to help."

Ant's defenses melted a little. "It's okay," he said, his voice quieting.

"It's just—my dad spent all summer telling me not to back down if someone is messing with me," Jamal said as they waited for the safety guard to signal them to cross. "You know, to stand my ground. To be strong. But when I talked to him the other day and told him why the fight started . . ." Jamal's gaze dropped to his feet. "He said that Ma wasn't worth fighting over."

"Whoa," Ant said. "For real?"

Jamal nodded. "But maybe he's right."

"No. She's your mom. Of course she's worth it!"

They began to cross the street. "So then you think I was right to jump RJ?"

"No, but . . ." Ant took a deep breath. "Still, what your dad said was kinda messed up."

"He's trying to be a good dad and everything now, but I can't forget about all the stuff he used to do."

Ant had overheard enough "grown-folks" conversations

to know that Jamal's dad had been *bad business* back in the day. Drugs, girls, gangs—you name it, he was into it. Some people even said that *he* was the one who dragged Jamal's momma down that path. It's bad enough when you screw up your own life, but it's just about unforgivable when you mess up someone else's.

"At least he's trying," Ant offered. "He's being honest with you."

"Whatever. Sometimes I wish I never knew about all the stuff he's done. What kid wants to hear that his dad was a junkie?"

"Well, *I* wish I knew more about Dad's past. About his drinking."

"Drugs are way worse," Jamal said. "I mean, at least alcohol is legal."

"I think they're both bad."

Jamal gave a limp shrug. "Eh. I guess."

Ant stopped walking. He was hoping for a lot more than that from his best friend.

Jamal turned around. "What?"

"Nothing."

"The way your hands are all balled up, something's bothering you."

Ant looked down. Sure enough, he'd formed two fists.

But what could youngblood say? Comparing problems never got anyone anywhere.

"Just . . . forget it," Ant said.

"Fine by me." Jamal straightened up. "Don't look now, but guess who's coming our way?"

Of course Ant glanced over his shoulder to see who was approaching.

*Shirley?*

She offered them a slight wave. "Ant, got a second?" she asked.

"Uh, yeah." He looked at Jamal. "Catch you later?"

"Sure," Jamal replied. He started toward school, wagging his eyebrows once Shirley couldn't see. I mean, the boy wasn't even discreet about it. He could have flagged down an airplane with as high as those brows were jumping.

Jamal headed toward a group of boys throwing a ball, leaving Ant standing there with Shirley.

Alone.

# CHAPTER 26

As Shirley took a step closer, Ant didn't know whether he should look directly at her or focus on something else. But her eyes were so big, so brown, so *wide* that it was almost impossible to look at anything *but* them. Eventually, he settled for staring at the tip of her nose.

He had to admit, that was kinda nice, too.

"I need to apologize about something," she began as she tugged at one of her tight twists. "I'm sorry about making fun of you the other day. You know, when we were playing cards."

"You already apologized."

"No. Technically, I just said I wouldn't do it anymore." She pulled on another twist. "So I'm sorry. I could tell how much it bothered you."

"It was fine."

She let out a sputter of laughter. "Please. You can hide things pretty well—except when it comes to that. You crack every time someone mentions your height."

Ant crossed his arms. "So do you."

Shirley opened her mouth but didn't say anything for a second. Then she nodded. "I know. It was nice of you to not make fun of me, especially when I was making fun of you."

Ant felt like he was on one of those shows where people are punking you and secretly recording it. "Did someone make you apologize to me or something?"

Instead of answering, Shirley reached into her pocket and pulled out a crumpled one-dollar bill. "Also, I need to return this."

"What . . . ?" he began, even as he reached for the money. His fingers lightly brushed against Shirley's hand, and he felt like he'd been zapped with one million volts of electricity. But in a good way.

"It's from my brother," she said, thumbing toward the playground.

Ant zeroed in on the kid who'd shaken him down in the gym climbing a rope ladder. "*Bobby's* your brother?"

"Yeah, he's a hustler in the making. But my dad

says that he's not allowed to swindle kids at school."

"I guess those rules don't apply to his sister." Ant grinned. "You know, you're good enough to play in the Oak Grove Spades Tournament next weekend. As long as you don't stack the deck."

Now Shirley was smiling. "Yeah, I heard more about the tournament. And I'm sorry for cheating the other day. My mom taught me that move with the deck. But I'm not supposed to use it in a real game. I only did it because you guys were talking *so* much trash."

"Jamal was the one doing the talking," Ant said.

"Yeah, but rotten pears come in pairs." When Ant frowned at her, she added, "I know—it doesn't make any sense. It was something my granddad used to say."

"I had a granddad who said stuff like that, too. But I don't like pears."

"Me neither."

They stood there, awkwardly running out of fruit to discuss.

"Anyway, that's it," she said finally. "Catch you in class."

Shirley headed for the building. Ant watched her for two, maybe three seconds, before sprinting after her. "*Are* you thinking about playing in the tournament next weekend?"

She stopped and shrugged. "I doubt it. I mean, I like spades, but I don't have a partner."

"You don't want to play with Terrence?"

"No, he mentioned that he's going to be out of town," she said. "And, well, if I played, I'd want a chance at winning. No offense to Terrence."

Ant took a deep breath and reached way down inside of himself to find a little crumb of courage. "Well, I was just wondering . . . would you be interested in playing . . . with me?"

Shirley raised an eyebrow. "What about Jamal?"

"He can't play. The fight, remember?"

"Oh yeah." Her face twisted up for a moment as she stewed it over. "I guess it could be kind of fun."

"Okay, it's a date." Ant cringed. "I mean, a deal!"

If Shirley noticed his slip-up, she didn't say anything. "Hold on. First, I have to ask my parents. I think they'll say yes, but—"

"It's a really cool festival," Ant said. "The spades tournament is just part of it. There's also a band and food. And there's a dunking booth and . . ." Ant's voice trailed off as he watched Shirley pull out a pen and open up her palm.

"Give me your number," she said. "I'll call you tonight if my parents say yes."

It took poor Ant three tries, but my man was eventually able to stutter out his phone number.

The bell rang just as Shirley was scribbling down the last digit. "I'll text you mine later today," she said as she started toward the school's front steps. "And, Ant—thanks for asking."

Since they were in the same class and all, Ant probably should have fallen into step beside her. But that just seemed weird. What else were they supposed to talk about? Apples? But he'd probably stumble over that, too.

Plus, he was worried how walking in together would look. He didn't want anyone to think that he *like*-liked Shirley.

Whether it was true or not.

# CHAPTER 27

By the time Ant got to class, most of the other students had partnered up for another of Mr. Reese's early morning game-without-a-prize activities. Terrence and Shirley were already in a corner, looking at something that Mr. Reese had posted to the wall. Ant felt a little pang of jealousy but quickly stuffed it down.

He ended up working with Dwayne. Halfway through the activity, Rochelle nudged him and asked, "You and Shirley are playing in the tournament together?"

"Um . . . yeah," Ant said. "Maybe."

Five minutes later, Marco asked the same thing. Only this time, the question came with a sneer.

By the end of the activity, news about Shirley and Ant playing in the tournament had spread throughout the class like brown gravy over a mound of mashed potatoes. And by the time recess came around, it had spilled over to other classes.

The worst taunts came during recess, from RJ, who had only been given one day of ISS since, technically, he hadn't been the one to start the fight. But with the way he kept trying to bait Ant, it seemed he hadn't really learned his lesson. Ant was starting to understand why Jamal had gotten angry enough to throw the first punch. RJ did not know when to back off.

"Dude, I can't believe you're gonna play with Shirley," RJ said. "You must really be hard up for a partner."

"What's wrong with her?" Ant asked.

"Nothing, I guess," said RJ. "But, I mean, you're never gonna win. Girls can't even play spades. Everyone knows that." A slow grin spread across RJ's face. "You just want her to be your girlfriend, don't you?"

"No, I don't!" Ant said. Which, of course, made things worse.

Now, Ant *knew* that he wasn't supposed to be talking trash. He did *not* want to go back to Mrs. Booker's office anytime soon—and especially the week before the tournament. Plus, let's be honest, he wasn't exactly the best trash talker in the world. Not by a long shot.

But he was smart.

Ant cleared his throat. "Man, you're just mad because you and Cordell are going to lose. *Again.*" He looked around at the kids who were starting to listen in. "Yo mama is so . . . um . . ."

Ant tried to look like he was thinking up an insult. But the truth was, he didn't have to actually *say* anything. RJ was more than ready to jump in.

"That all you got?" RJ shot back. "Yo mama's so stupid, she thought a quarterback was a refund."

RJ's comeback was feeble, but it got a few laughs, especially from the boys.

"What are you laughing at?" Ant said to Dwayne. "Didn't you hear what RJ said about yo mama?"

Dwayne frowned. "Well, RJ's mama's so skinny, her elbows touch!"

"Nah, man," spat RJ. "Yo mama's so dumb, she tried to give cheese to her computer mouse. Yo mama's so ugly, people dress up like *her* for Halloween. Yo mama's sooooo stupid . . ."

As RJ kept piling on Dwayne, Ant slowly backed himself up out of the group.

Ant may not have been the biggest, strongest, or wittiest guy, but guess what?

It don't matter if your opponent is a master at checkers if the game you're playing is chess.

# CHAPTER 28

Ant figured that once the final school bell rang, he should probably go outside and meet Jamal. Tell him about Shirley before anyone else did. But the boy couldn't bring himself to do it. He didn't want to listen to any more nonsense.

He knew how he was acting by avoiding the confrontation—*weak*. Still, Ant found himself fighting through the crowded hallway to get to the library instead of the school's double-door exit. He found a quiet table by the windows and stayed there for a while, flipping through a few graphic novels.

Twenty minutes later, when he finally left the building, all the students—including Jamal—were gone.

At home, Ant grabbed his phone and headed straight to his room. The house was empty—his dad must've decided not to work from home after all—but Ant needed plenty of privacy. He didn't want either of his parents overhearing his conversation.

"So you done hanging up on people?" Aaron asked before Ant even had a chance to say hello.

Ant winced. He'd been so wrapped up with everything else, he'd forgotten about their last call. "We had, um, a bad connection."

"Yeah, right," Aaron said. "Hang tight. I'm going to call you back." A few seconds later, Ant's phone was asking him to accept a video chat.

Ant tried to hold back his smile as his brother's face popped onto the screen. He liked to joke that Aaron was the goofier-looking of the two of them, but he was mighty glad to see that goofy face.

"So what were you saying?" Aaron snapped his fingers. "Oh yeah! You were apologizing."

"Okay. Fine. I'm sorry for hanging up on you. But you shouldn't have said that I was little."

"Fair point. For the record, though, you said sorry first."

"Aaron!"

"I'm joking!" he said. "But what's up?"

Ant hesitated. He honestly didn't know where to start.

Aaron really was a good older brother, because he knew exactly what Ant's confused, frustrated look meant. "Okay, tell me about school. How are things there? How's Jamal?"

"He's fine, I guess. But . . . his brother said something to me the other day." Ant took a breath. "Taj said that I should have had Jamal's back during that fight."

Aaron rolled his eyes. "Taj doesn't know what he's talking about."

"But what if *you* were in a fight? Wouldn't you want me to help?"

"First of all, I play the flute. I'm not exactly the fighting type. Fists don't ever solve anything anyway."

"But what if someone jumped you? For no reason?"

"Why would that happen?" Aaron stroked the barely-there stubble on his chin as he considered the possibility. "Maybe if a girl's ex-boyfriend got jealous of my superior looks . . ."

"I'm being serious, Aaron. If that happens, what am I supposed to do?"

Aaron scrunched up his nose. "Ant, I don't know what to say. Sure, if I got jumped, and no one else was around, and it was ten guys on one, then okay, maybe I wouldn't mind a little help. But you only fight if you absolutely *have* to." He brought the phone closer to his face. "Was the only way to help Jamal getting physical?"

"No, I guess not."

"There you go. Why are you listening to Taj, anyway? He might seem cool and all, but he wouldn't know the difference between right and wrong if he read it in a dictionary."

Maybe Taj had been right about one thing—Aaron *was* kind of a poindexter. Ant cracked a smile.

"What's so funny?"

"Oh, nothing," Ant said. "It's just, Taj doesn't think you're the best at giving advice, especially when it comes to girls." Ant leaned back. "By the way, did Nia *friend-zone* you?"

"No! We just happened to be better off as friends." Aaron scowled. "What do you even know about girls and dating?"

"Apparently not much more than you."

"Tell me this," Aaron said. "Why are *you* talking to Taj about girls?"

"Well, um, since Jamal had to drop out of the tournament, I had to find a new partner. And I found a good one. But she's a girl. Her name is Shirley." Ant thought about describing her black twists of hair, or her high cheekbones, or her mahogany-brown skin, but he didn't need another reason for his older brother to tease him. "The kids at school are trying to say that I *like* her or something. Just because I asked her to be my partner."

"That's stupid," Aaron said. "Then again, you do look like you're blushing."

"I am not," Ant said as his cheeks got even redder.

"I thought Black people couldn't blush," Aaron said. "You learn something new every day."

"Aaron! I don't like her!"

"You mean you hate her?"

"No! I like her. But not *like*-like. I *kinda* like her. You know, *medium*-like her."

"She's not a steak," Aaron said. "But it's cool. I remember when I fell in love for the first time. I was at band camp—"

"I am *not* in love!!"

"Dude, why are you yelling?"

"I . . . I . . ." Ant didn't quite know how to answer.

Aaron laughed. "Alright, I'll leave you alone. What else is going on? How's Ma?"

"She's good," Ant said. "She's been working the early shift all week."

"Yeah, it pays a little better," Aaron said.

The boys were quiet for a moment.

"Okay," Aaron said. "How are things with Dad?"

Ant shook his head. "It's probably nothing . . ."

"Ant—"

"Does drinking grapefruit juice mean that you're an alcoholic?"

Aaron's mouth dropped open. For a second, Ant thought that maybe the phone had frozen.

Then his brother started laughing again. "Where did you get *that* idea from?"

Now Ant was really blushing. "See, I told you it was nothing . . ."

"No, no," Aaron said, struggling to regain his composure. "I mean, I never heard of grapefruit juice being a slippery slope toward alcohol, but hey—what do I know? I only scored 1500 on the SAT."

"I'm hanging up," Ant said.

"Okay, I'm sorry. I'm just messing with you," Aaron said as he finally calmed down. "To be honest, I've been worried. I thought he might be gambling again or something. But if he just has a grapefruit juice habit, everything is fine."

Ant didn't say anything.

"He's *not* gambling, right?" Aaron's eyes narrowed as he

leaned forward. Ant could almost feel his brother's gaze burning a hole through the screen. "Right?!"

"I promised," Ant began, his voice barely a squeak. "I told him that I wouldn't tell Ma."

He'd thought it would feel good to share this with someone.

He was wrong.

"Ant! You can't keep something like that from her!"

"I didn't know—"

"You're not a baby. Think for once!"

"Why is gambling such a big deal anyway?" Ant yelled back.

"Because—" Aaron froze again. Then he tried to put on his own poker face. "Don't worry about it."

"What are you not telling me?"

"Don't worry about it," he repeated. "I'm going to call Ma tonight. She needs to know."

"No! I promised I . . ." Ant shook his head. That wasn't going to work. "At least wait until tomorrow. She's pulling a double shift. You'll just stress her out."

Aaron studied his brother, looking for a crack in his armor.

Looking for the smallest hint of a lie.

But Ant was a Joplin man. He had learned how to

keep a straight face from the best of the best.

"Okay," Aaron finally said. "But I'm calling first thing in the morning. And don't tell Dad. He'll just lie about it."

"I won't," Ant said. "I promise."

The baby card shark had already fibbed plenty of times that day. Who was one more lie going to hurt?

# CHAPTER 29

Ant hated setting his alarm clock for four thirty in the morning, but he wanted to make sure that he didn't oversleep. He hadn't quite worked out all the logistics yet, but he figured that if he got up right after his mom left for work, he could warn his dad about what was coming before Aaron told her about the gambling. The way Ant saw it, if his father came clean—if he was honest with Ant's mom about everything—then things just might blow over. I mean, when he was a kid, his parents told him that it was always better to be honest than to try to hide something. If it was true for him, it had to be true for his dad, too, right?

But for better or worse, Ant didn't have to wait until four thirty to find out.

The keyboard clicking started up at 2:00 a.m.

Ant crept down the hallway, then placed his ear to his parents' bedroom door. He could hear the faint rise and fall of his mother's breath.

That was pretty bold of Roland, starting his gambling before Yolanda left for work. Maybe that meant he'd already fessed up. But if I know Roland—and I *do* know Roland—it probably just meant he was getting more reckless.

Youngblood stood in front of Aaron's closed door, hoping his dad was emailing a client or writing up new ads for his business. But deep down inside, he knew what was really going on.

*Please be wrong, please be wrong, please be wrong,* he told himself.

Then he pushed open the door, so fast that it banged against the wall.

"Ant!" his father whispered loudly. His laptop sat on the bed beside him, and a very full glass of *something* bobbled in his hands. "What in the— What are you doing up?!"

"I couldn't sleep." Technically, that wasn't a lie.

"Boy, get back to bed."

"How's the game going?" Ant asked. "Are you up or in the hole?"

"Anthony, can we discuss this tomorrow? I'm right in

the middle of a hand." His dad looked down at the screen, and accidentally tipped his glass, spilling some of his drink on the bedspread. "Now look what you made me do!"

"I'll help you clean it up," Ant said, stepping forward.

"No, no," his father said. "Just go back to—" The laptop beeped, and once again, his father looked at the screen. "Ant! You made me 'check' automatically. I was going to fold!" He took a long swig of his drink. "If I lose this hand because of you . . ."

Ant waited for his father to finish. His dad had never really made empty threats like that before. At least he hoped it was empty.

*Where did my dad go?* Ant wondered.

Ant strongly considered moonwalking right out of that room. He could get back underneath his sheets, squeeze his eyes shut, and pretend that none of this had ever happened. Maybe his brother wouldn't call their mother. Or if he did, maybe it *was* better if she dealt with this.

His father picked up his laptop. "Anything else? If not, go to bed."

Ant's mouth opened, but nothing came out. His hands were balled up so tight, the boy was liable to cut off the circulation in his fingers. He watched his father take another long draw of his drink and start another game.

"I said, go to bed, Anthony."

Ant relaxed his fingers. His spine softened. He couldn't do it. Couldn't be man enough to face the problem head-on.

All he wanted to do was run away.

"Yes, sir," Ant finally said, his voice meek. "Good night."

Ant turned to leave, then almost jumped out of his skin. "Ma!" he yelled.

His mother stood at the door, taking everything in. His father. The laptop. The glass.

The creases around her eyes were deep as valleys.

"Yolanda." His father took a breath. "How long have you been standing there?"

"Long enough."

"Listen," Roland began. "I don't know what you heard, but—"

"Go on to your room, Ant," his mom said. "And close the door behind you."

As Ant retreated, he told himself that this was good. His mom finally knew what was going on. And he hadn't been the one to squeal to her. He hadn't done anything wrong.

Unfortunately, his heart didn't agree.

# CHAPTER 30

To their credit, Ant couldn't hear his parents yelling at each other. But it was hard to miss the sound of Aaron's bedroom door slamming. Or the kitchen door. Or the trunks and drawers and refrigerator and just about everything else that could be slammed.

Then came the feet pounding down the hallway. The slam of another door. The roar of his father's car engine as it peeled out of the driveway.

And then the scariest sound of all: silence. One that seemed to stretch into forever.

Eventually, like a tortoise poking its head out of its shell, Ant emerged from his room.

He found his mother sitting at the kitchen table, still wearing her pajamas, a coffee cup in her hands. The creases around her eyes were even deeper than before.

"Ma?" Ant asked.

Yolanda motioned for Ant to join her. "Your father's gone," she said, her voice steady. "I asked him to leave."

Ant looked down at the table, unsure of what to do. What to say. What to even think. He wished he had something to do with his hands. Some food to stuff into his mouth. Anything to stop his mind from focusing on his mother's words.

"For how long? A couple of days?" Ant asked, his words full of hope.

"I don't know. I . . . don't want to set a deadline." His mother took a sip of coffee. "He's going to call you later. Maybe in a day or two."

Ant kept staring at the tabletop.

"You know none of this is your fault, right?"

He shrugged.

"Look at me, Anthony." She waited until their eyes were locked. "None of this is your fault. *None.* If anything, it's mine. I should have seen the signs." She sighed. "For a guy with a struggling business, your father seemed pretty flush with cash all of a sudden. And as for the drinking, I had a feeling about that, too."

Ant sat up. "He was really drinking?"

She nodded. "His trunk is full of liquor bottles. There are probably more at his office."

Ant blinked, willing himself not to cry. He did *not* want to break. To be weak. Not now.

"I'm so glad I overheard you talking," she continued. "If you hadn't woken me up, there's no telling how long this would have gone on."

That didn't make Ant feel better at all. It wasn't like he'd *planned* on waking her up. He had wanted to figure this problem out for himself—to get his father to confess—before getting his mother involved.

She downed the rest of her coffee. "Sweetie, how much do you remember about when your dad was drinking? You know . . . *before?*"

Ant thought about it. "Not much. My first real memory of him is of us walking to school on the first day of kindergarten."

His mom smiled, and for a second, all those creases and wrinkles melted away. "He was so happy. So proud of you! And you loved him so much. It was easy for you to accept your father coming back home. Both you boys."

"Dad told me that he never went to one of those treatment centers." Ant began to trace invisible words into the table with his index finger. "But then how did he stop drinking? Where was he? Six weeks is a long time to be gone."

Ant's mother watched as his fingers fluttered across the table. "Your father wasn't gone for six weeks," she finally said. "He was gone for two years."

Ant's eyes sprang open. "Wait. What? But—"

"I know. He just couldn't give it up. And I couldn't let him stay. Drinking—it can change a person. Turn them into someone you barely recognize. You were so little when he left, and somewhere along the way, you heard that famous celebrities go to those clinics for six weeks to get over their addictions. I wasn't brave enough to burst your bubble."

"You all knew. And you *lied* about it?"

"I'm sorry. It's just . . ." She took his hand. "You looked up to your father so, so much. He loved that. He *needed* that. I think we were all worried it would have destroyed him if you knew the truth. That maybe it would have destroyed you, too."

Ant wanted to be mad at his mother, but she was right. Knowing that his father cared more about drinking than getting back to his family would have crushed him back then. Shoot—it was crushing him now. "So where was he for those two years?"

"Bouncing around. Sometimes he'd stay with your grandparents, or sleep at his office. He even stayed with Jasper for a while, which, of course, was a complete disaster." She picked up her coffee mug and rose from the table. "I didn't give up on your father. I never stopped loving him. But I couldn't trust him anymore. He wasn't the man I married."

That made Ant think about his father's unspoken threat earlier that morning. He stood up and slowly followed his mom to the counter. "Ma, you have to tell me the truth. Did Dad ever . . . well . . ." His heart ached even *thinking* the words. "Did he ever . . . hurt you?"

She fiercely shook her head. "Ant, I promise. Your daddy's not a violent man. Sure, we would argue, but he never hit me. He'd never raise his hand to any of us."

"Then what happened? Why was the drinking and gambling so bad you couldn't live with it?"

Ant's mother took a long time to pour herself a new cup of coffee.

"Ma. Please."

"Are you tired?" she asked. "You don't have to go to school today if you don't want to."

Ant knew what that meant. No more talk about Dad's past. "Are you going to work?"

"I don't think I have it in me. Not today. But maybe I'll pull a double this weekend to make up for it."

Ant glanced at his mother's hospital ID card in its usual spot on the counter. "Is money going to be an issue with Dad gone?"

"I have some money saved up for a rainy day, and Aaron can apply for a scholarship for next semester if money gets really tight."

"Next semester?! Dad will be gone that long?"

"Let's not get ahead of ourselves," she said. "All I'm trying to say is that I don't want you worrying." She tapped his nose. "So if you win that spades tournament, the money is yours to keep. Not that winning is important. I just want you to—"

*"Have fun,"* Ant said. "Got it." He clenched his teeth. The spades tournament was the last thing he wanted to talk about. "I'm going to lie down. I think my brain is too scrambled to focus on school today."

"Speaking of scrambled . . . let me know if you want some eggs later on."

Ant didn't have it in him to make a joke about his momma's cooking. "Sure thing, Ma."

A million thoughts swirled around in his head, and one kept forcing its way to the surface—*was Dad gone for good?*

But there was no way Ant could ask his momma a question like that. He didn't want to put her on the spot. But more than that, he was afraid she'd already made up her mind.

And he just couldn't take any more disappointment.

# CHAPTER 31

Ant spent most of that morning drifting in and out of sleep. And even though I'm supposed to be hands-off—just a storyteller, a Joplin family historian if you like—I couldn't help humming a few lullabies from up above, hoping the sweet melodies would soothe that boy. Because if anyone deserved a slice of peace, it was Ant.

He may have been a little too afraid of confrontation, but there was nothing weak about how he was handling the cracks in his family. No sir, not at all.

Around lunchtime, he got up and fixed himself a sandwich, then sat down at the kitchen table and actually got started on his schoolwork.

All the while, he kept his phone near in case his father texted.

Instead he got one from Jamal. **Hey! I heard that you and long legs are partners? That true? Why didn't you tell me?**

The next came from his brother. **I talked to Ma. Don't feel bad about Dad. It had to happen.**

Ant was lower than a two of clubs. He needing something—*anything*—to break his way. Then all of a sudden his phone started ringing.

When he glanced at the screen to see who was calling, Ant started sweating like a snowman in a hot tub, even though the house was a cool seventy-three degrees.

It was Shirley.

He picked up the phone and pressed it to his ear. "Hello?"

"Oh. Hey, Ant," Shirley said. "You weren't at school today." Then she laughed. "Duh. And water is wet, right?"

"Did I miss anything?" Ant asked.

"Not really. Mr. Reese tried to rap the South Carolina state song to us, but it's probably better that you missed that."

For the first time that day, Ant laughed.

"So," she continued. "I just wanted to, um, check to see if you were sick or something. 'Cause my parents said that we could be partners in the tournament."

"Oh! That's great! And I'm not really sick. I'm just—"

The words got caught in his throat. *What was he supposed to say?* "I'm good," he finally sputtered out. "Better now that I know you'll play with me."

Then he frowned. *I sound like such a dork.*

"I was thinking," Shirley said, "maybe I could come over tomorrow and we would practice—"

"No!" Ant's armpits smelled like swamp water. "I mean, I can come to you, Shirley."

There was a pause as Shirley pulled the phone away to ask if that was okay. "Sure," she said after a moment. "One o'clock?"

"That works." Ant started searching for a pencil. "Let me just write down your address . . ."

"I know where they live," his mom said from the doorway.

Ant glanced at his mother over his shoulder. He wondered how long she'd been standing there.

"Um, scratch that," Ant said. "My mom knows how to get to your house."

"So I'll see you tomorrow?" Shirley asked.

"Yeah. See you then." Ant pulled the phone closer to his mouth. "And thanks for calling."

He hung up, and looked at his mom again. "Why are you staring at me?" he asked.

She smiled. “No reason.”

He wasn’t sure he believed her. But as he got up to get a glass of water, there was a little bounce in his step.

Shirley’s call didn’t bring Ant the slice of peace I thought he deserved, but I’m guessing that he didn’t mind so much.

# CHAPTER 32

Unfortunately, that was the only bit of good news that Ant received that day.

His father didn't come home. He didn't call, either.

And when Ant texted Aaron, his brother just kept repeating the same things over and over and over again:

**It's going to be okay.**

**It's not your fault.**

**Both Ma and Dad are going to be okay.**

**It's not your fault.**

**I love you.**

**It's not your fault.**

All pretty words. All as useful as a tuxedo on a bullfrog.

The next morning, Ant's mother declared it the start of a new era. A new beginning. She said that she and Aaron and Ant needed to keep living their lives. That they couldn't let Roland's absence change who they were.

Which, of course, meant that she was gonna keep babying Ant, whether he wanted it or not.

"You don't have to drive me to Shirley's house," he said as he followed his mother outside that afternoon. "It's less than a ten-minute walk."

"Boy, hush and get in the car," his mom said. "I won't embarrass you in front of your friend. I just want to see mine."

His friend—make that *partner*—was indeed the daughter of Joanie Mae Brockington, now known as Joan Heyward. Shirley's mom had grown up in Oak Grove—right alongside Yolanda and Roland and Anita Booker.

"Joanie Mae left for the military right after high school, but she's home for good, now that she's retired," Ant's mom explained as they got in the car.

Once she'd set the radio to the old R & B station and backed out of the carport, she turned her attention to Ant. "You know, now might be a good time for us to chat."

Ant braced himself, waiting for his mom to tell him that he shouldn't bring up his father's alcoholism with

Shirley. Or the gambling. Or that his mom had kicked his dad out.

"About yesterday . . ." she began.

"Yes?"

"When you were talking on the phone with Shirley, it reminded me of the conversation we had a few days ago, where you seemed, I don't know . . . worried about playing spades with a girl. Maybe because of how you might feel about her?"

Ant blinked hard. "We *so* don't need to talk about this."

"I teased your father about giving you his Big Talk on the first day of school, but he's right. You probably do have a lot of conflicting feelings *coursing* through your body, and—"

"Ma! Shirley and I are just friends!"

"You know, y'all had a playdate together once—years ago, when Joanie Mae was back home between postings. She and I joked that maybe y'all would end up dating each other. And look at you now."

"Ma . . ."

"Not that you're old enough to date, mind you. But I suppose you could go to the movies together, with a group."

Ant blushed so much, you could melt a marshmallow

on his cheeks. He'd almost rather be talking about his father than whatever this conversation had turned into.

His mom reached over and patted Ant's arm. "I just want you to know that if you ever want to discuss how you're feeling, you can always talk to me. Or Anita. Or—"

"Duly noted," Ant said, even saluting his mother. "Now can we please stop talking? We're almost there."

"Okay, baby."

Ant died all over again. "Please don't call me *baby* when we get there."

"Of course not, sweetie."

"Ma!"

"Not that either? Gotcha, puddin'."

"Now you're just messing with me!"

His mom pulled up in front of what Ant prayed was Shirley's house. "Okay, okay, I'm stopping. Let's go in and say hey."

But before they'd even made it up the driveway, Mrs. Heyward opened the door and rushed out to greet them. "Yolanda!"

"Joanie Mae!" Ant watched the women wrap their arms around each other, then do that sway-and-bounce-thing that old people always did when they hugged.

Then Mrs. Heyward gave Ant the once-over. "And look at you. The last time I saw you, you barely had any teeth." She opened her arms. "I'd love a hug—that is, if you're okay with it."

Ant had never heard an adult ask if a kid wanted to be hugged. His aunts and uncles sure never did when they smooshed the life out of him or patted the top of his head. "Um . . . alright?"

Ant gave Mrs. Heyward a quick hug, then followed her into the house.

Shirley and a man who Ant assumed was her dad rose from the couch. The man walked toward Ant, sidestepping a small orange tabby lounging in the middle of the floor.

"I'm Kenneth Heyward," he said, shaking Ant's mother's hand. Then he stretched his hand toward Ant. "And you must be Anthony? Or do you prefer Ant?"

Mr. Heyward's handshake made Ant imagine what a wolf feels when it's stuck in a steel trap. "Nice to meet you, sir," he said. "Ant is fine."

"Hey, Ant," Shirley said, giving him a small wave from her spot in front of the couch. Her hair looked to be freshly twisted.

"We've been looking forward to your visit all morning," Mrs. Heyward said. "Shirley's been excited to—"

"Ant and I are going to the kitchen!" Shirley said, loud enough to make the cat scurry away.

Ant waved goodbye to his mom. "I'll call you before I head home."

"Okay, sweetie." After seeing the look of horror plastered on Ant's face, she quickly added, "Sorry, baby, I didn't mean—" She winced. "Sorry . . . *Anthony*."

Well . . . at least she hadn't called him *puddin'*!

# CHAPTER 33

The kitchen was down a hallway lined with photos of Shirley and her family. Ant noticed how the really old ones were only of Shirley and her mom. Then came Shirley's dad. And then Bobby.

A plate of brownies sat in the center of the kitchen table, right next to a pack of Unicycle playing cards.

"Did you know that we'd met before?" Ant asked as they sat down.

"Not until yesterday." Shirley cracked a smile.

"What are you grinning about?"

"Mom told me a lot of stories about your family—especially your grandfather." She slid the cards out of the box. "Like how he was this legendary gambler and—"

"Technically, he preferred *game enthusiast.*"

Shirley began to shuffle. "Mom also said that your grandfather ran the . . . what did she call it? . . . *the numbers racket*? And that *my* grandfather was happy to participate in it, though he usually lost."

Ant didn't know what was prettier—Shirley's smile, her brown fingers as they worked the deck, or the sound of the cards as she made a perfect shuffle. "Supposedly, Grandma made him quit when my dad was born," Ant said. "He started playing spades instead. Then he taught my dad. And Dad taught me and my brother. The tournament's sort of a family tradition."

"Now I see why you're so hard-core when it comes to spades. I didn't know your entire family legacy was on the line if you don't win."

Ant picked up a brownie. "It's not *that* big of a deal."

"Says the boy who carries around a deck of cards, even at school."

"The boy who *used* to carry around a deck of cards," Ant said. He bit into his brownie. "And that was Jamal's pack."

"That reminds me—how did Jamal take it when you told him we were playing together?" Shirley's eyes took on a glint of mischief. "Give me all the details. Was he crushed? Did he cry?"

Ant kept right on chewing like that brownie was the best one that had ever been baked.

"You didn't tell him, did you?"

Ant shrugged. "Well, I didn't know for sure that you were going to agree until yesterday. And it's not like you told Terrence."

"Yeah, I did," she said. "On Thursday morning. Didn't you notice how quiet he was?"

"I just thought he'd finally run out of questions to ask. Besides, he's missing the tournament anyway, right? So why would he care if you play with someone who actually has a shot to win?"

"Don't be mean," she said.

"Like you're not mean about Jamal?"

"Yeah, but it's different. You're too nice to be mean." She went back to shuffling. "Plus, Terrence was hurt. I'm not sure, but I think he has a crush on me."

Of course, Ant's throat chose right then to choke on a bit of brownie.

"You okay?" she asked as Ant sputtered out a few feeble coughs. "Want something to drink?"

"I'm fine." Ant wiped his watering eyes with the back of his hand. "So . . . do you, like, have a crush on him, too?"

"NOOOO!" she yelled, way louder than necessary.

"I mean, Terrence is nice. Well, not nice like you are. I mean . . . what I'm saying is . . ." She cleared her throat. "No, I don't like him like that."

"Okay," Ant said.

"Okay," she said back.

Ant picked up another brownie, and Shirley went back to shuffling the cards. "How long has the tournament been going on?" she asked.

"Oh, I don't know," he said, trying to play it cool. "I can't really remember."

She just looked at him.

"Fine," Ant said after a moment. "This year is the twenty-second anniversary of the tournament. My dad and granddad played together four times, winning each time. Dad played and won three more times with our cousin. And my brother won twice in a row. Not that I'm counting."

She whistled. "Sounds like you're counting to me," she said. "So how did you and Jamal do last year?"

Ant sighed. "It was my first time competing. Jamal and I . . . could have done better." He picked at his thumbnail. "We got bounced in the first round."

"Ouch."

"I reneged near the end of the game. We were going to lose anyway. I was hoping the other team wouldn't catch it. But that made it worse because then it looked like I didn't know what I was doing."

She tsked. "Cheaters never win."

"Says the girl who beat me by stacking the deck," Ant said. "Anyway, are you going to quiz me all day, or are we going to play?"

"Good point," she said. "Bobby! Where are you?"

A few seconds later, her brother burst into the kitchen and made a beeline for the brownies. "What happened to all the—" He looked at the crumbs on the table in front of Ant and pouted. "How come he gets to eat them? Just because you have a—"

"Fine! Take a brownie!" Shirley yelled. Then she took a breath, composed herself, and said, "I figured we'd start with a game against Dad and Bobby, just to see how it feels to play as a team. Then we'll talk strategy."

"Sounds good to me," Ant said. "But I thought your mom was the spades player in the family."

"Oh, we're nowhere close to being ready to play against my mom."

"She's that good?"

"I'm *way* better than good," Mrs. Heyward said as she entered the kitchen. She paused at the table and looked at her daughter. "You told Ant about my rules, right?"

"I was just getting to that." Shirley cleared her throat. "So . . . Mom said I could play, but only if I promised not to talk any trash."

"Not at all?" he asked.

"Not at all," Mrs. Heyward repeated.

Like I've said all along—Ant was not a good trash talker. But he'd grown up around it. It was part of the game. And spades without trash talk was like bacon without the grease. Like Gladys Knight without the Pips. Like Dr. J without an Afro. It just wasn't right.

But if Ant wanted to play with Shirley, he didn't really have any other choice.

He nodded. "Okay, I guess. But do you mind me asking why?"

Shirley put down the cards. "Mrs. Booker. Once she found out that Jamal and that other boy's fight started because of some trash talk, she kept digging and worked her way back to our game on Monday. She called me and Terrence into her office yesterday morning. I told her that we weren't talking *that* much trash, but Terrence had a different opinion." She shook her head. "He really does talk too much."

"You know what they say." Bobby snickered. "Snitches get stitches."

Ant's mouth dropped open as Mrs. Heyward whipped

her head toward her son. "Boy, where did you hear that?"

He shrugged. "Dad."

"I swear," she mumbled. "I'll have a conversation with your father later. Now go wash your face. You look like you've been flossing with brownie crust."

All of a sudden, Ant wondered if he had brownie bits stuck in his teeth, too. He looked down at the table and ran his tongue over his front teeth.

"So anyway, that's why we can't talk any trash."

"I wonder if Mrs. Booker is going to call me back to her office on Monday."

"I wouldn't worry about that." Shirley smiled. "After I told her that the only thing you did was call me *Miss Texas*, she agreed that that was too tame for you to get into more trouble over."

"Ugh," Ant said. "But thanks."

"And I'll just add, this isn't the first time that Shirley's gotten in trouble due to trash talk," her mother said. "But she assured me that this would be the *last* time. Right, Shirley?"

Shirley quickly nodded. "Yes, ma'am."

"Good." Mrs. Heyward picked up the cards, then started cutting them, all with one hand.

"Show-off," Shirley whispered.

"Just trying to set the tone," her mother shot back. She plopped the cards on the table. "And sit up, Shirley. Ain't nothing wrong with being tall."

As Shirley straightened up, her cheeks turned pink, purple, and red, all at once.

Mrs. Heyward then winked at Ant. "You agree with me, don't you?"

"Um, yes, ma'am," he said. "I like tall. I mean, there's nothing wrong with . . . I mean . . ." Ant sighed.

Mrs. Heyward laughed, and Shirley crossed her arms. "Can you get Dad now? Or is there anything else?"

"Just one more thing," her mother said. "Your partner's got brownie stuck in his teeth."

# CHAPTER 34

Ant was many things. Confident in his playing skills. Kind to his friends. Charismatic—in his dreams, at least. And *completely* wrong about how he'd been playing cards for the past year.

I mean, Ant and Jamal were a good pair. But Ant always had to overcompensate for Jamal's little mistakes—playing the wrong suit, playing too high a card, cutting too early, overbidding. With Shirley, it was so much easier. She almost always put down the right card. She knew how to read the board and to remember who played what. Being Shirley's partner was like playing with a darker, smarter, cuter version of his brother—which sounds downright horrible, now that I think about it.

An hour later, after calling his mother to make sure it

was okay, Ant and Shirley walked over to the Quick Mart to register.

"Whatcha know good, Ant?" Mr. Eugene asked from his usual perch. Casey, Ellis, and Selmon nodded in their direction.

Then Mr. Casey frowned. "Well, well! Who's the little miss you got with you?" he asked.

Shirley stepped forward. "I'm Shirley Heyward."

Mr. Ellis scratched his head. "I don't know any Heywards. You know any Heywards, Selmon?"

Mr. Selmon scrunched up his face. "Was sticky-fingered Fred a Heyward or a Harvey?" He turned to Shirley. "Who are your people?"

"My mom is Joan—er, Joanie Mae Heyward," Shirley replied. "Used to be Brockington."

All three men slapped their dominoes down on the table. "Yeah! Little Joanie Mae!" Mr. Casey said. "She was a firecracker, that one. Always ready to tell you what was on her mind—whether you wanted to know or not."

"She's back from the service now, right?" Mr. Ellis asked. "What was it, navy?"

"Army," Shirley said.

"Yeah, yeah," Mr. Selmon said. "She was the pride of

Old Jethro's eye . . ." He slid his hat from his head. "May he rest in peace."

The men closed their eyes and bowed their heads for all of three seconds. Then Mr. Ellis said, "Now that I think about it, that joker owed me twenty dollars before he died."

Mr. Selmon swatted Mr. Ellis with his hat. "You can't bring that up," he said. "She could still be in mourning."

"He died over five years ago!" Mr. Ellis said. "How long am I supposed to wait until I get my money back?"

"If you geniuses could be quiet for a few minutes, these young'uns and I have more pressing issues to discuss." Mr. Eugene waved Ant and Shirley over to him. "What can I help you with today?"

"I'm here to swap out partners for the tournament," Ant said.

"Yeah, we heard about Jamal getting into a fight with Chucky Muldrow's boy," Mr. Eugene said. "But I got some bad news for you, slick. I don't think we have enough entrants for a youth tournament this year."

Ant stood there for a moment, letting Mr. Eugene's words sink in.

"We were already low, but the city is putting on some fancy video-game festival on the same day, and a few teams dropped out," he continued as he looked through his notebook. "Seems like kids would rather plug themselves into a computer and fire make-believe bullets at each other than play a game that requires real skill."

"Are you sure?" Ant asked. "Maybe I can find some kids to—"

"Son, we're out of time. You'd have to get at least five other teams to join by tomorrow." He shook his head. "I just don't think you can pull it off."

"Well, thank you. I guess there's always next year," Shirley said as she patted Ant's shoulder. The boy was so down, he didn't even notice it.

Mr. Ellis chuckled from the domino table. "Tell 'em about Florida, Gene."

Mr. Eugene fiddled with the pages of his notebook. "I'm retiring at the end of the year," he said. "My daughter wants me to move down to Miami Gardens with her and her family. Said it'd be better for my joints."

"So this is the last year of the tournament?" Ant asked. All he could see was the look on his father's face as Aaron held up that trophy.

"To be honest, interest has been waning for a while." Mr. Eugene tapped his fingers on the countertop. "Y'all want a piece of candy? Free of charge."

"What? Gene is giving out *free* candy?" Mr. Selmon said. "That fool must be going senile."

Ant started to walk off toward the candy aisle, but Shirley remained in place. "What about the other divisions?" she asked. "Do the teens have enough teams to play?"

"Yeah, they surprised me." Mr. Eugene squinted. "Wait. Why are you asking?"

Ant rushed back to the counter. The teen tournament would be harder, but the prize money was way more! Five hundred dollars! "We can play with them!"

"Look, kids—"

"Mr. Eugene, aren't you always saying that spades is spades and skill is skill?" Ant said.

"He got you on that one, Gene," Mr. Ellis said.

Shirley nodded. "Plus, don't you think it's a little *ageist* to say that we can't play with the teens? That's like saying I can't play because I'm a girl."

"Yep, you're definitely Joanie Mae's kid," Mr. Casey added.

Mr. Eugene sighed. "It ain't just about skill. Those teenagers—well, they can be all-out ruthless. I don't want you to get your feelings hurt."

Shirley planted her hands on her hips. "You think I'm

afraid of a little trash talk just because I'm a girl?"

No one said anything. Ant was thankful that none of them told her who Mr. Eugene was really talking about when it came to hurt feelings.

"We'll take our chances," Ant said quietly.

"Yeah," Shirley added.

"Go on, let 'em play," Mr. Ellis said. "What doesn't kill you makes you stronger." He cleared his throat. "And if she wins, maybe I'll get my twenty dollars back."

"Ellis!" all of the men yelled.

Mr. Eugene flipped to a new page and pushed the notebook toward Ant. "I hope you know what you're doing."

Ant started to write down their info but stopped. "We need a team name."

It was tournament tradition for every team to come up with an unusual—and boisterous—name. The funnier the better.

"What were you and Jamal?" Shirley asked.

"The Flaming Jalapeños," Ant said.

"And y'all sure 'nuff flamed out last year, didn't you," Mr. Casey said, slapping his hand on his knee.

Ant ignored Mr. Casey. "We need something good."

"And something quick," Mr. Eugene said. "I got customers to tend to."

Ant spun around and took in the empty store.

"What?" Mr. Eugene said. "They could be coming in any second."

"Why can't it be something plain, like Joplin and Heyward?" Shirley asked.

"You might as well call yourself White Rice," Mr. Selmon said. "What about Big Joker and Little Joker? You know, since one of you is so tall, and the other so small?"

That didn't seem funny to Ant. Or Shirley.

Shirley snapped her fingers. "I got it! What about the Antagonists? You know, *Ant*-agonist?"

"Isn't that one of those people who digs up mummies?" Mr. Casey said.

"That's an *archaeologist,*" Ant and Shirley said at the same time. Then Ant added, "Antagonists are bad guys."

"Not always," Shirley said. "An antagonist is just someone who is opposed to the main character of a story." She crossed her arms. "Anyway, heroism is a construct."

"You're weird, you know that."

"True. All the best people are." Shirley straightened her shoulders. "Plus, Antoinette is my middle name so it works for both of us."

"I have no idea what either of y'all are saying."

Mr. Eugene pointed to the paper. "Just write your stuff down."

As Ant scrawled their name in the notebook, Shirley said, "I'm going to grab a soda. Be right back."

Ant nodded. Then his eyes drifted to the old video poker machine in the corner. The machine had sat there—unused—for as long as Ant could remember, with a coat of dust to prove it.

"Does that machine still work?" Ant asked.

"Oh, no. That thing hasn't been plugged in for ages. The state outlawed video poker years ago." Mr. Eugene leaned closer. "Why are you asking?"

"Oh, no reason," Ant said. "Just curious."

Mr. Eugene glanced at the men sitting at the domino table. They kept their eyes on their dominoes, doing their best to pretend that they weren't eavesdropping.

"It's just, you aren't the only person asking about that old machine this week." Mr. Eugene pulled two lollipops from behind the counter. "I reckon that's the problem with gambling—if you want to do it bad enough, you'll eventually find somebody to accommodate you."

Ant didn't look at Mr. Eugene as he took the candy. "This person who asked about it earlier . . . had he been drinking?"

After what seemed like a thousand hours, Mr. Eugene said, "Son, I'm honestly not sure. But I do know that things probably feel real tough for you right now. Word travels fast in the Grove, you know. But you're always welcome to hang out here, if you need to get away."

"Always welcome," Mr. Ellis chimed in.

"For sure," Mr. Casey added.

"Thank you," Ant said softly. Then he heard Shirley coming up behind him.

As she walked up to the counter, Ant wondered if she'd overheard what they'd been talking about. But if she had, she didn't say anything about it.

'Cause sometimes the best kind of partner was a silent one.

# CHAPTER 35

On the walk home, Ant was feeling okay. Happy, even. (Of course, that lollipop didn't hurt.) But as soon as he stepped foot inside his house, he couldn't help noticing the echoes of his father everywhere. They made him feel all ground up and raw on the inside.

And it wasn't just him. His mother was struggling as well. Ant would find her in the kitchen, staring off into space, her black coffee cold. Or he'd catch her in the living room watching the channel guide scroll endlessly on the TV screen.

They even skipped church on Sunday morning. Usually, it took a natural disaster for that to happen. But then again, they almost always went as a family. If Ant and his momma showed up alone, people might ask questions they weren't ready to answer.

Ant had told Shirley he'd try to come over again so they could get a little more practice in, but now he was thinking that maybe he'd be better off with his mother. Of course, Yolanda sniffed out his plan as soon as he even hinted at it and said he could either go to Shirley's house to play spades or he could stay home and help her scrub the floor.

Ant cared for his momma right fiercely, but he was also a ten-year-old kid. There was no way he was voluntarily scrubbing any floors.

But before he left, he called his brother to tell him to check on their mom.

"She'll be okay," Aaron said. "She's strong. And she's been through this before, remember?"

"How did y'all deal last time? I can't stop thinking about him."

"I know. I was the same way," Aaron said. "Maybe you should talk to someone."

"You mean like a counselor?" Ant thought about it for a moment. "I don't know. Do we really want anyone knowing our business?"

"If you try to hold all the worries in, you'll explode. I think maybe that's what caused Dad so much trouble."

"I guess."

"Can you at least talk to your friends? Jamal or the new girl?"

"No way!" Ant shook his head hard. "I can't tell her. She'll just feel sorry for me."

Now, Aaron could have taken a potshot at Ant. Could've joked about how he liked the smart girl with the mahogany-brown skin, or how he needed to step up and not be so afraid. But again, more times than not, Aaron was a pretty good older brother.

"Just think about it, alright?" he asked.

"Okay," Ant said. "I will."

And he did.

# CHAPTER 36

"Shirley, your *friend* is here!" Bobby yelled from the Heywards' front door.

"Bobby! Stop yelling!" Shirley yelled back.

Ant wondered if he had ever been so annoying. Aaron and his friends probably thought so. Ant figured he probably owed them all an apology.

"You hungry?" Mr. Heyward asked as Ant entered the kitchen. Shirley sat beside him at the table. "We just ate, but there are plenty of leftovers. The only rule is—you have to say three nice things about the food before you trash it."

Ant sniffed the air. "Mrs. Heyward baked a ham?"

"Right meal, wrong person," Shirley said.

Ant looked at Mr. Heyward. "*You* cooked?"

"Don't act so surprised," he said. "Surely you don't think that only women can cook."

"Oh, no, sir!" Ant said, pumping out his chest. "I helped my mom make dinner the other night!"

Shirley rolled her eyes. "Helping was the least you could do. I mean, you ate, right?"

Ant cleared his throat, eager to change the subject. "So where'd Bobby run off to? Is he playing with us?"

"Nope. You graduated to the big leagues," Mr. Heyward said. "Joan will be out in a moment."

"Just don't forget, no trash talk," Shirley warned.

Ant nodded, even though he was pretty sure that *he* wasn't the one who needed the reminder.

For a woman who loved spades, Ant was a little surprised that Mrs. Heyward didn't care for the hard-core trash talk that usually accompanied it. But don't be mistaken—that didn't mean she didn't like to brag. The only problem was, the more she bragged, the more *competitive* Ant's partner became.

Not that it really mattered. Joanie Mae beat those kids like a pair of runny eggs.

"Alright, let's wrap this up," she said at the end of the first hand as she slapped her last cards—the king, the queen, and the ten of spades—on the table. "We'll go ahead and take those last three books."

"How is that not trash talk?" Ant asked as he pushed his cards toward her.

Mrs. Heyward shot him one of those sweet but deadly Southern smiles. "I didn't say anything negative about you. I didn't call you any names. I'm just stating a matter of fact."

"It sure felt negative," Ant mumbled.

"All things considered, you and Shirley did pretty well, given that y'all have only been playing together since yesterday." Shirley's mother started counting off on her fingers. "First, you both did a good job of bidding. You forced me to play my king of clubs, which Shirley cut to win a book. And y'all went on that nice run during the middle of the hand." Her voice was encouraging, but even Ant could tell she had more to add.

"Okay, that's three. Let's have it," Shirley said. "What'd we do wrong?"

Mrs. Heyward looked at Ant. "What do you think Shirley could have done differently?"

"Ma'am?" Ant glanced back and forth between Shirley and her mother, unsure which of them he should try to appease.

"Oh, come on, Ant. I know you noticed it. I saw you scowl when it happened."

That boy didn't know that his ever-so-dependable poker face always went on the fritz whenever Shirley was around.

Mrs. Heyward picked up one of the books in Shirley's stack and spread it out across the table. "You cut your partner, Shirley. His ten of hearts would have walked, but instead you played your four of spades."

"Um, I think I was afraid that you were going to cut to win the hand," Shirley said.

"Yes, but I was playing last," her mom replied. "I was going to have to cut anyway if I wanted to win it."

Shirley tried again. "Well, if you were going to cut, I wanted to make you jump for it. If you really wanted the book, I wanted to force you to play a high card."

"With a four of spades?" Mrs. Heyward laughed. "I wouldn't have had to jump very high, would I?"

"I, um . . . I thought—" Ant had rarely seen Shirley fumble so much.

"It's okay, sweetie," her mom said. "I know you cut your partner because you wanted to control the next turn. You didn't think he was going to play what you wanted—and you wanted to win." Mrs. Heyward rose from the table. "I know you're still working on building up trust. Shoot—I've been married to your father for almost nine years, and I still don't trust him."

"Hey! You owe me three nice things!" Mr. Heyward said, playfully swatting at her as she passed.

"What's the deal with the three things?" Ant asked.

Mr. Heyward leaned back in his chair. "If you hadn't noticed, Shirley's mom can be a bit blunt sometimes. So when we got married, we made a deal. She has to say three nice things about a topic before she's allowed to criticize it. But if she keeps this up, we're going to have to add a fourth!"

"I heard that!" Mrs. Heyward yelled from down the hallway.

Shirley's father stood. "I'm going to check on Bobby. He's a little too quiet for my liking. Anybody need anything while I'm up?"

Both Ant and Shirley shook their head.

"Your mom's really good," Ant said once her father left. "Did she learn to play in the . . . ?"

Ant stopped talking once he noticed that Shirley wasn't paying attention. Instead, she was flipping over the cards on the table, pile by pile, and whispering to herself.

"Mom's right," she finally said.

"It's not like we were going to win," Ant said. "Plus, I've had to do the same to Jamal before."

"Yeah, but I should know better." She looked at Ant. "I'm sorry for not having faith in you."

Ant thought back to what Shirley's mom had said about trust issues. He was starting to wonder if she was talking about more than spades.

Shirley began pulling the cards into a pile. "Speaking of Jamal, have you manned up and told him that we're partners?"

Ant knew that Shirley was joking, but even so, he had to force himself to laugh. "He heard but we haven't talked about it."

"You really should," she said. "I mean, how would you feel if he picked another partner without telling you?"

"Why are you so worried about Jamal?" Ant asked.

"I just . . ." She paused, then sighed. "I don't want him confronting you about it at school on Monday," she said. "He's kind of mean, Ant."

"He's my best friend."

"Fine. He's a mean best friend."

Ant crossed his arms. "It wasn't like you were all that nice when we first met you."

"I only picked on y'all because he picked on me first,"

she said. "He pushed my buttons. But why did he have to start making fun of *you*?"

"You don't understand him," Ant said.

"Maybe you don't either."

They were both quiet for a long moment, glaring at each other from across the table.

"Are y'all finished arguing?" Mrs. Heyward said as she and her husband appeared in the doorway.

"We weren't arguing," Shirley said. "And I can't believe y'all were spying on us!"

"Sweetie, you assume that you have the right to privacy. But this is our house, remember? And no, we weren't eavesdropping. Not on purpose, anyway." Her mother sat down. "If y'all are going to win that tournament, you need to stop arguing and start playing like a team."

"They've only been partners for a minute," Mr. Heyward said.

"Yeah, but they've been pals for a lifetime." She picked up the cards. "I still remember the first time you two played together . . ."

Shirley's eyes twitched. "Mom!"

"You should have seen 'em, Kenny. Chasing each other all around the park. Though they were more interested in hugging and loving on each other than climbing the playscape."

Ant's face turned hotter than jalapeños dipped in Tabasco sauce.

"Shoot, me and Yolanda had to pry them away from each other. I've never seen two babies put that many kisses on each other in my—"

"Can we play cards?" Shirley yelled.

"I think it's my deal," Ant said just as quickly, reaching for the cards.

Mrs. Heyward smiled as she handed over the deck. "Look at that. Y'all *can* work as a team."

# CHAPTER 37

Despite the mortifying stories, Ant really enjoyed playing cards with Shirley and her family. It kinda reminded him of how things used to be at his house.

When it was time to leave, Shirley walked him to the door.

"Thanks for having me over," he said. "It was really fun."

"My parents are *embarrassing*, not fun."

"Well, my parents are . . ." Ant froze. He didn't know if he could talk about his mom and dad like he used to. How could so much have changed in just a handful of days?

"Anyway," he began again, his voice quieter. "You want to practice tomorrow after school? Back here?"

"Sure. But I wouldn't mind going up against your dad at some point. I want to see how good the legend is."

She made a fist, but Ant couldn't bump it. Instead, he rubbed the back of his head. "Maybe one day. But this week is bad." He took a step backward. "See you tomorrow."

It seemed Shirley wasn't the only one with trust issues.

But Shirley *was* right about one thing. Ant needed to talk to Jamal about his new partner. So he made a detour on the way home.

*Maybe I can talk to him about Dad, too. We are best friends, after all.* If there was anyone that Ant could trust, it was Jamal.

When he got to Jamal's house, he found Taj out front, messing with something underneath the hood of his car. "Hey, Taj," Ant said. "Is Jamal home?"

Taj stood and looked Ant up and down. "You're in luck—Rebbie just stepped out." He wiped his hands with a rag that was even dirtier than his oil-slicked palms. "So what you been up to? Hanging out at your girlfriend's house? Or is that your *partner's* house?"

Ant's gulped. "So you heard."

"Yeah, we both heard." He spat on the ground, then

wiped his mouth with the back of his hand. "That was a straight-up punk move. The least you could have done was told him. I mean, talk about *weak*."

"But I wasn't even at school on Friday," Ant said. "It wasn't a done deal until then."

Taj sucked his teeth. "Knowing you, you probably skipped so you wouldn't have to own up to it and face him like a man."

"That's not why I wasn't there!"

"Whatever. Truth is, Jamal is way more over it than I am. I guess he's always known you're *soft*."

Ant could feel the pressure building up behind his eyes. *Not here,* he told himself. *Not here.*

Just then, the car horn in Taj's old hooptie started blaring all on its own. Kinda like it was touched by an angel. Or a ghost.

Hmm . . . fancy that.

Taj stepped away to look back underneath the hood. "You might as well go on up," he said. "At least you have enough guts to talk to him now."

Ant slowly made his way to the door, and with each step, the pressure behind his eyes diminished. He took a deep breath and knocked. Jamal might be mad, but this was his best friend, right? He'd understand.

A few seconds later, Jamal appeared at the door. "What are you doing here?"

Ant couldn't help but notice how much taller Jamal seemed. "I'm here to apologize," Ant said. "I should have told you—"

"Yeah, you should have," Jamal said, stepping outside onto the porch. "I had to hear it from Terrence of all people. And you chose *her*? You've been different ever since she showed up." Then he shrugged. "But it's cool. I got me a new partner, too."

"Really? I thought you weren't allowed to play."

He shrugged again. "When Taj went by the Quick Mart this morning to register his usual team, he heard that Mr. Eugene was letting kids our age play in the teen tournament. So he dropped Vic so we could partner up."

Ant badly wanted to ask why it was okay for Taj to get a new partner and not him, but he knew better than to step on that landmine.

"That's great!" Ant said. "I'm just surprised Rebbie's letting you play."

"What she don't know won't hurt her." Jamal's eyes narrowed. "And you'd *better* not tell her."

"I—I won't," Ant stammered. "But don't you think—"

"You know how big the prize is," he said. "Rebbie will get over being mad if we win."

Ant had known Rebbie as long as he'd known Jamal. And that was a false statement if he'd ever heard one.

Jamal took a step toward the door. "I need to get back inside. I'll see you in class tomorrow, Ant."

"Wait. Jamal!" Ant looked up at his friend. "Are we cool?"

Jamal thought a second, then said, "Yeah. We're cool, little buddy. And we'll be even better once me and Taj lay a beatdown on you and your girlfriend in the tournament."

Ant was so shocked, he didn't know how to reply.

But it was just as well. Jamal was already gone, the screen door slamming shut behind him.

# CHAPTER 38

On Monday morning, Ant woke to find his mother again sitting in the kitchen, a huge mug of coffee on the table in front of her. But this time, she'd also fixed a full breakfast of French toast and bacon for Ant.

"Thanks, but you didn't have to do this," Ant said as he sat down. "Aren't you going to be late for work?"

"I cut back my hours this week. You know, while we acclimate to your father not being here."

Ant was surprised by how normal she sounded. Like it was a fact she'd already accepted—hook, line, and sinker.

"Go ahead and eat," his mother said. "I tried a new seasoning."

As Ant took a bite of the French toast—which was cold—he thought about the "Joanie Mae" rule. "It's flavored really well," Ant said. "And it's the right texture—not too hard, not too mushy. Plus, that bacon looks really crisp."

"Good Lord. Do I look so hard up for a compliment that I need my child to lay it on that thick? Not that I'm complaining, mind you."

"It's something I learned from Shirley's dad. You're supposed to say three nice things before you say something critical."

Her eyebrows furrowed. "You want to register a complaint?"

Ant just shoveled another bite of French toast into his mouth.

"Smart kid," she said. "It seems like you and Shirley are really hitting it off. I know you're supposed to be going over to her house most of this week, but tomorrow is out. You're going to Anita's house for the afternoon."

"You mean Mrs. Booker?"

"Ant, you don't have to call her that outside of school. She's known you since you were a baby. Changed your diaper and everything."

"Don't remind me."

"Your father and I talked last night."

Ant was glad he had that French toast to stuff in his mouth.

"Tomorrow, he's coming over to pick up a few things. Some clothes. Maybe some furniture." Ant's mother reached over and put her hand on his. "Stop eating for a second, and talk to me."

Ant looked at his mom's hand. "So Dad's moving out. Like, for real?"

"Yeah. We both need space to think things through. I need him to promise to go to a treatment center. A real one. That's the only way he's going to get his drinking and gambling under control."

"And then he can come back home?"

She pulled her hand back. "And then . . . we'll see. Right now, he doesn't even realize that he has a problem."

Ant started tearing his bacon into smaller pieces. "But why do I have to go to Mrs. Booker's house? Can't I just stay at Shirley's?"

"I don't know how long it will take. Your daddy didn't tell me exactly what time he's coming over." She sighed. "Plus, I thought you might want to talk to Anita about this whole thing."

"She knows?"

His mom nodded.

Ant broke off another piece of bacon. "Why can't I be here when he comes by? I'll stay out of the way."

"Sweetie, I have no idea what shape your father will be in when—*if*—he shows up. And until I know for certain that your father is getting help, you can't see him. He knows that, and he agreed to it. Maybe in a month or so—"

"A month?" Ant shook his head. "What about the spades tournament? It's in less than a week. He's got to be coming to—"

Ant stopped.

He didn't have to continue.

He could already see the answer on his mother's stone-cold face.

# CHAPTER 39

Ant couldn't believe it.

His father was going to miss the tournament.

The *last* tournament.

What was the point in playing if his dad wasn't going to be there to see him win? Or even compete.

Ant wanted the look his dad had given Aaron when he won. The one that made it seem like he was going to burst because he was so happy, so *proud* of his kid.

Ant wasn't going to get that. For sure, not for the tournament. And if his father didn't get better, he might *never* see that look again.

He might never see his *father* again.

As the day wore on, Ant's sadness slowly transformed into smoldering anger, though Ant wasn't sure who to direct it at. Maybe Aaron for making Ant deal with all of this on his own. Maybe his mom for ignoring her suspicions and forcing Ant to be the bad guy.

No, mainly he was angry at his dad for causing all this trouble in the first place. *Do as I say, not as I do.* Wasn't that the line he always quoted? Ant was supposed to be a man. Toughen himself up. Deal with his problems directly. But his dad used drinking and gambling to do just the opposite. It wasn't fair.

Ant's anger even spilled over to his classmates. He snapped at Terrence when the boy asked one too many questions about the math homework Mr. Reese had assigned. And Ant was especially brutal during a football game at recess, doing his best to throw the ball *through* people whenever it left his hands.

Jamal was back in class, but he went out of his way to avoid Ant. Which was just peachy as far as Ant was concerned. He didn't want to talk to Jamal, either. Because if Jamal tried to make one of those snide jokes about Ant being small, he wasn't sure what he would do.

Shirley must have noticed the anger radiating off of him, because she did a pretty good job of avoiding Ant, too. It wasn't until after the last bell rang that she finally asked, "Are you alright?"

"Of course! Why wouldn't I be?"

"O*kay*," she said. "Jeez."

As Ant followed her out of the door, he switched on his phone. No new messages. *Dad spends who knows how long doing all of the things Ma told him not to, but* now *he's decided to follow the rules?*

Outside, Bobby bounced up and down as he waited for them with the other second graders. "Ant's coming over today? Cool!" He rubbed his hands together. "Time for another beatdown."

Ant narrowed his eyes.

"What's wrong with him?" Bobby asked Shirley.

"Nothing!" Ant said. "I'm fine!"

Shirley glared at Ant, opened her mouth like she was going to say something, then shook her head. "Come on, let's go," she said, picking up the pace.

Bobby struggled to keep up, while Ant purposely lagged behind. He didn't know why he was even going over to Shirley's house. There was hardly anything to play for.

Honestly, Ant was in a pretty bad place. I whispered words of encouragement to him. Youngblood definitely needed them. But when you're that steamed, you don't want to hear nothing but the angry buzz of self-pity in your ears. You don't want to see anything except red.

Once they turned the corner, Bobby took off down the sidewalk. And by the time they reached the house, he had disappeared inside. Shirley, however, remained out front.

"What in the world is wrong with you?" she asked Ant.

"I said it was nothing."

"If you're going to be like this, maybe we shouldn't practice today."

"Maybe we shouldn't practice at all!"

"You're the one who wanted to do all this practicing in the first place."

"Then just forget it," Ant said. "Let's not even play."

Shirley planted her hands on her hips. "Does this have anything to do with Jamal? I heard he signed up for the tournament."

"This ain't about him. He's playing with his brother."

She threw her hands up. "Then what is it?"

"It's nothing," he said, turning to go. "I'll see you at school tomorrow."

"Ant! Wait."

He stopped walking.

"What's really going on?" Shirley's voice had lost its edge. "I'm okay with not practicing, but it seems like something is bothering you. You didn't drink your chocolate milk today. You *always* drink your chocolate milk."

"How do you know that?" he asked.

Shirley shrugged.

She didn't realize it, but she was making it mighty hard for Ant to stay angry. But he couldn't talk to her about his dad. Not yet.

"I'm sorry for yelling," he said. "It was a bad day."

"You know you can tell me *anything*. And I won't judge you."

"I know," he said. "Really, I'll be back to my usual self soon. I just need . . . a day off."

She looked at him for a long time, before nodding. "So I guess I'll see you tomorrow?"

Her question hung there in the air between them until Ant nodded. "Yeah. Tomorrow."

Shirley gave him a small smile and scurried up the driveway.

Ant started off toward home. But after only a few steps, he stopped to look back at the house. He'd never met anyone quite like Shirley.

And he wasn't one hundred percent sure, but it kinda looked like the curtain in the side window jerked shut just as he'd turned around. Someone was watching him. Making sure he was okay.

He really hoped it wasn't their cat.

# CHAPTER 40

Ant hated coming home to an empty house.

He sat down at the kitchen table so he wouldn't have to pass by his parents' room and unzipped his backpack.

But after a few minutes of staring at his math textbook, he found himself glancing at his phone.

The last text his father had sent him was about something silly, a meme he'd seen online a few weeks earlier. And by his number, there was his picture, all smiles.

Ant typed out a message, then deleted it. He wasn't going to text his father. His *dad* was the adult. If someone was supposed to reach out first, it should be him.

But deep down, Ant knew that wasn't the only reason he was hesitating. He'd made a promise. He was supposed to be his dad's partner. And he'd let him down.

Ant had let his mom down, too. He should have said something the first time he'd caught his dad playing poker. If he'd stepped up and made a decision earlier he could have avoided disappointing one of his parents. Instead he'd disappointed them both.

Here's the thing—Ant was a ten-year-old trying to solve grown people's problems. Aaron had told him that he hadn't done anything wrong. So had his mother. But at that moment, Ant refused to hear otherwise.

Then his phone buzzed with a message from Shirley.

**Hey, Ant. You sure you're okay?**

**Yeah. Sorry about earlier.**
**I was in a pretty bad mood.**

**Yeah. And water is wet.**

Ant's whole body shook with laughter.

**I'll be better tomorrow. Promise.**

Then, feeling a little bold in the britches, he added:

**I really like playing with you.**

**We make a good team.**

He stopped, squinted at his phone, then erased the note.

Then he typed it in again.

His thumb hovered over the SEND button, frozen in place, when a plastic cup in the dish rack fell into the sink, clattering against a dirty plate. The sound scared the bejesus out of poor Ant, and his arm jerked hard enough to accidentally press SEND.

Hmm. That was a mighty odd phenomenon, wasn't it?

Ant watched in horror as the message was delivered, then read. A few seconds later, the phone buzzed.

**I really like playing with you, too.**

**We make a GREAT team.**

Ant gathered up his books and walked down the hallway to his room. And he was grinning so hard, he didn't realize he'd walked by his parents' bedroom until he already passed it.

# CHAPTER 41

The next morning, Ant was running late. The warning bell had already rung by the time he got to school, so he headed straight to class. And would you believe it? The first thing he saw when he walked through the door was Shirley and Jamal talking to each other over by the window. It was kinda like catching the Loch Ness monster and Beyoncé sharing tea and crumpets. Some things just weren't supposed to exist in the same universe.

"Hey, Ant," Jamal said, "I was just telling Shirley about the tournament last year. You know, how you reneged and lost the game, and then ran off—"

"Jamal!" Ant said.

"And I was telling him no one cares about last year," Shirley said. "Except, of course, that it's a good thing that you upgraded partners. Now you don't have to worry about reneging in the first place."

Mr. Reese walked over to them. "Let's take our seats, people," he said. "And remember, *everyone's* a winner in the game of life."

Shirley looked at that man like he was a few cards short of a full deck, before shaking her head and walking toward her desk.

Ant caught up to her. "Yeah, I know. Mr. Reese is weird. But at least he's nice." Then he lowered his voice. "So what happened to the 'no trash talk' rule?"

"What? You think I was exaggerating about how good I am?"

"Fair point." Ant hesitated. "Listen, that stuff Jamal said about me running off—"

"I wasn't even listening to him," Shirley interrupted. "So, we're still good for after school?"

"Yep!" Then Ant frowned. "Oh! Actually, I can't meet today after all. My, uh, parents are going to be busy tonight, so they wanted me to stay with a family friend. I even brought a change of clothes, just in case I have to sleep over. But everything will be back to normal by tomorrow."

"Oh, okay." She arched an eyebrow. "You're sure?"

"Positive."

Ant didn't really believe that, but it was nice to say, anyway.

"I'll be with you in a second, Mr. Joplin." Mrs. Booker poked her head out of her office and flashed a smile. "Just have a seat."

Ant slumped into one of the lime-green chairs. He didn't mind going to Mrs. Booker's house—he'd been there plenty of times before. But he didn't exactly want anyone to see him.

Getting teased about Shirley would be a cakewalk compared to what he'd have to face if his classmates saw him riding shotgun in Mrs. Booker's car.

After a few moments, the door opened. "Thanks for stopping by," Mrs. Booker told a fourth grader named Alisha Watkins as they came out into the hall. Then Mrs. Booker held out her arms.

Alisha smiled, almost gratefully, and gave her a quick hug.

"Now hurry on to the after-school program. You can always come back tomorrow if you want to talk again." Then she turned to Ant. "Come on in, Ant. I just need to finish packing up my things, and we can get out of here."

"You just called me Ant," he said as he followed her inside.

"Of course I did. It's your name, right?"

"But you never call me Ant."

"Not during school hours." She looked at her watch. "But now that I'm officially off the clock, I'm no longer your assistant principal. I'm just your auntie Anita."

She sure still *looked* like an assistant principal.

"Try me," she continued. "Tell me something that you would never tell *Mrs.* Booker. I promise, I won't get mad."

"Well . . ." Ant thought for a moment. "I yelled at Terrence yesterday. For asking too many questions."

She stifled a smile. "I can understand how that could happen. He's quite . . . inquisitive. Anything else?"

"Um, last week, a kid—not me, of course—was telling corny 'Yo Mama' jokes during recess."

"If you're going to tell jokes like that, they *have* to be good." Her eyes danced. "But at least it's better than calling someone Miss Texas."

Ant sat up. "Hey!"

"Go on. Tell me something else" She steepled her fingers together. "It doesn't have to be about school. It can be about the spades tournament, about your brother, anything."

Ant shook his head. He didn't just fall off the turnip truck. He knew where she was going with all those questions, and he wasn't about to let himself get duped.

"You know, your mom really loves you. This is hard for her, too."

"I know."

"And your father loves you, even though—"

"Really, I'm good," he sputtered. "I don't need to talk about it."

"Okay. Just give me five more minutes." She turned her attention to the papers on her desk. Then she picked up a folder, revealing a book called *My Body! My Rules!* underneath.

Ant couldn't help staring at it. Mrs. Booker—that is, Anita—cleared her throat. "You can borrow it if you want."

"No, that's okay."

"It's a book about consent," she explained. "You know how you're supposed to ask before trying to kiss or hug or even touch anyone."

Ant nodded. "Yeah, I knew that."

"Good," she said.

Ant thought about how Shirley's mother had asked for a hug, instead of just grabbing him like other adults often did. "Are you *always* supposed to ask for consent?"

She looked him dead in the eye. "Yep."

"Like, even married people."

"Yes. But there are different ways to ask. Just now, when I held open my arms to Alisha and let her come to me? That's another way to ask for consent. I let her make the final decision."

Ant tugged on his ear. He repositioned himself in his seat. Then he scratched at a dry patch of skin underneath the band of his sock. "Let's say you wanted to hold someone's hand. If you just offer your hand out to them, and they take it . . ."

"That's a way to ask," Mrs. Booker said. "But sometimes it's better to say what you want out loud." She put her pen down. "Some people find the direct approach quite romantic."

"Whoa, whoa," he said. "Who said anything about romance?"

"I'm sorry. I didn't mean to imply anything. I assumed we were talking hypothetically."

Ant narrowed his eyes. This conversation was starting to smell like a chunk of ripe tuna. "Did my mom ask you to talk to me about girls or something?"

"Of course not," she said. "But I know that you and

Shirley have become good friends. She's quite bright, isn't she?"

Ant waited for her to go on complimenting Shirley. Maybe about how she always had the right answer in math. Or how she knew the capitals of every state. Or how it would be okay if Ant was indeed interested in her. My man knew grown-ups sometimes went fishing for information with a baited hook.

Instead, Anita rose from her desk. "I'm finished. We can head home." She opened her file cabinet and pulled out her purse. "Maybe after dinner, you and I can teach my boys how to play spades?"

"Sure," Ant said. He could use the practice with anyone who'd play with him, even littles like Justin and Devon.

But deep down he knew he'd spend the whole time thinking about someone else. Someone he'd much rather partner with.

# CHAPTER 42

It turned out that Ant and Mrs. Booker didn't have time to get in a hand of spades after all. Ant's daddy had come by while Ant was at school and Yolanda was at work to collect most of his belongings. On the way home from the Bookers', Ant's momma didn't outright bad-mouth Roland, but the scowl on her face spoke volumes about how she felt.

The following day, she changed the locks.

Ant tried to summon up the courage to text his dad again, but each time he tried, he deleted the message before sending it. What was he supposed to say? What *could* he say?

During a break in class on Wednesday, Ant went to the library to do some research on something that had been bugging him. He'd always thought alcoholics were all corner bums—folks who couldn't keep their jobs or even stand up straight most of the time. But he discovered that they could look like anyone—like Mr. Gramm *or* his father. A clean shirt and a big smile didn't mean someone didn't have a problem.

He also found out all sorts of information about organizations that help addicts, and even some for kids and other family members. It was reassuring to know that there were people out there who knew more about this stuff than he and his mom did. People who had been in his shoes. People they could go to if the situation with his dad got even worse.

Things still felt confusing by the time he went to Shirley's house for practice. They even beat her parents in a game—though Ant was too distracted to really enjoy it.

On Thursday, Ant's mother asked him to come home early so they could have a special mother-son dinner. Instead of cooking, they ordered Chinese food. Gobs and gobs of it. They were halfway through their second carton of shrimp fried rice when they heard a key sliding into the door.

Ant and his mom looked at each other.

The doorknob rattled but didn't turn. Then came the banging.

"Can't a guy come home and surprise his mom and baby brother?"

"Aaron?" Ant's mom muttered. She rushed to the door and unbolted it. "What are you doing home?"

Aaron couldn't have answered if he wanted to—his mom had locked him into the biggest bear hug possible. Ant noticed that his mother hadn't asked if it was okay, but Aaron didn't seem to mind.

Once she let him go, Aaron opened his arms to his brother. "What? Too big for hugs now?"

Ant found himself flying toward his brother and launching himself at Aaron's wiry frame. Then he pulled back. "Aren't you supposed to be at school?"

"I only have one mandatory class on Friday, and my teacher told me I could make up the work next week." He stepped back outside, then waved at someone on the street. "Donnie was planning to come home as well, so they gave me a ride."

"Why didn't you tell me?" his mom asked.

"'Cause I knew you'd say not to come." He sniffed the air. "Is that shrimp fried rice?"

As Aaron dropped his stuff off in his room, Ant began

to hope that maybe *now* everything would start returning to normal. If anyone had a plan for how to help their dad, it would be Aaron.

His brother returned to the kitchen and started piling food on his plate. "Kind of early for dinner, isn't it?"

"I just wanted to spend some time with Ant," their mother said, still beaming. "And now I get to spend time with both of my boys. Though you almost made me jump out of my skin when you tried to open the door."

"Yeah, sorry. You changed the locks?" When she nodded, he put down his fork. "How are you holding up?"

"Better now that you're here," she said.

"I called him, you know," Aaron began. "I wanted him to know how mad I was. I wanted him to know that he couldn't—"

"Aaron." Yolanda shot a sideways look at Ant. "Maybe we should talk about this after dinner."

Ant stared at his brother. "You talked to Dad? What did he say?"

"*He* didn't say anything," Aaron replied. "I told him to leave us alone."

His mother pushed her plate away. "I wish you hadn't called him when you were upset."

"Why aren't *you* upset?" Aaron asked. "He promised

that he wouldn't drink again, Ma! He *promised*!" Aaron crumpled up the paper napkin in his hand. "And then to find out that he was gambling, too? It's just like before."

Ant shook his head. "Aaron, I know you're mad, but come on! He's our dad. So what if he made a mistake? You want to throw me out as soon as I make one, too?"

Aaron rolled his eyes. "Stop being dramatic. What Dad did before wasn't some stupid mistake—"

"Enough," Yolanda snapped. "Roland messed up, and he's gone. That's that. And maybe we're better off without him."

Ant could feel that old, familiar pressure building behind his eyes. He knew he was going to cry, but he pushed ahead anyway. "I was reading up about alcoholics at school," Ant said as his eyes became glassy. "It's a disease, you know. But he can get help. *We* can help him! He's our dad! It's what we're supposed to do!"

Yolanda took Ant's hand. "I know you love your father. We all do. And he does need help. But he has to be willing to take it. This isn't the first time that he's lost control. We just can't trust him yet."

Ant felt the tears sliding down his cheeks. He pulled away from his mother and rose from the table. "I'm not hungry. Can I be excused?"

Aaron's scowl finally disappeared. "Ant, don't—"

"It's okay," his mother said. "Let him go."

As Ant ran down the hallway, he realized Aaron coming home hadn't changed anything. Nothing was normal.

And maybe it never would be again.

# CHAPTER 43

Ant went to his room and flopped onto the bed. Then he got under the sheets with his school clothes still on—a big no-no. But at that moment, Ant wasn't interested in following the rules.

He grabbed his phone, hoping to see that he'd gotten a text from his father while they were in the kitchen talking about him like he was a lost cause.

Before he'd even thought it through, he fired off one of his own.

**Hey Dad**

Ten seconds later, Ant's phone buzzed. But not with a regular call. With a video chat.

Roland Joplin *never* video chatted.

"Dad?" Ant answered.

"Hey, buddy!" his father said, talking from what looked to be his office. "How are you?"

Ant was expecting his dad to look, well, different. Strange. Drunk. But other than a few extra bags underneath his eyes, he looked just like he was supposed to. He was even sporting that famous grin.

"I'm good, Dad. What about you?"

"I miss you. Your mom and brother, too."

"He's here, you know. Aaron."

"What? That's great!" Then there was a pause and for a second—a *blip*—his daddy's smile broke. Ant wondered if his father was thinking about the last conversation he'd had with Aaron.

"I'm sorry that you and your brother are stuck in the middle of this little spat between me and your momma. But things will blow over soon."

"Where are you staying?" Ant asked, eager to change the subject. "Did you find an apartment nearby?"

"No way am I going to spend money on an apartment, just to break the lease in a couple of weeks," he said. "Now, look. I know I messed up. I own up to that. But things will be fine once your momma knows I'm serious about quitting. The drinking *and* the gambling."

Ant sat up. "You're going to rehab?"

"Naw. It's not as bad as all that," he said. "I'm quitting cold turkey on my own. Haven't had a drink since Friday. Speaking of which—you were right to say something about it like you did. If anything, you should have done it sooner." He winked. "Sometimes, you got to call out your partner when they make a bad play, right?"

Ant managed to give a small head nod. The thing was, his daddy praising him didn't make him feel any better. If anything, it did the opposite.

"I can't wait to see you," his father continued, his smile back at full wattage. "Maybe on Saturday."

Ant's heart leapt up like an overcaffeinated jackrabbit. "You mean at the tournament? You'll be there?! I thought . . . Ma said—"

"Oh, don't worry about her," he said. "But hey, when I ran into Mr. Eugene's store last week, he mentioned that he didn't think he'd have enough kids for you and Jamal to play against."

Ant blinked a few times as he processed what his father was saying. He realized that he hadn't even talked to his father about Shirley. *How could so much happen in a week?*

"It's a shame, too," his father said. "I was looking

forward to seeing you compete." Then his eyes brightened. "Is Aaron competing? Is that why he's back?"

"I think it's too late for Aaron to enter. The deadline was—"

"Maybe Mr. Eugene will make an exception," his father said, bowling right over Ant's words. "I mean, Aaron's the reigning champion! Two years in a row!" He rubbed his chin. "It would have been something special to see *both* my boys in the tournament again."

Ant paused.

Maybe he *could* make his father's wish come true.

"Mr. Eugene is letting me play with the older teens." Ant took a deep breath. "That's why Aaron's back. He's my partner."

"What? Really?" he asked. "What about Jamal? I don't want you to kick your partner to the curb. You know, like some people do."

Ant winced. He knew that was directed at his mom. "Jamal is playing with his brother, which means I get to play with mine."

*All technically true,* Ant reminded himself.

"So what do you think, Dad?" Ant asked.

Ant's father leaned back in his chair. "I wouldn't miss it for anything in the world."

"You know . . . Ma'll be there, right?"

His father held up his hand. "I'll be on my best behavior. I swear." He stood, his grin darn near eclipsing everything else on the screen. "My boys teaming up! The Joplin men against the world. I'm so proud of you!"

Ant smiled back. But all he could think about was what he'd just done to Shirley.

And that *didn't* make him feel very proud.

Not at all.

# CHAPTER 44

"Ma, I know it's a school night, but I really need to run by Shirley's house." Ant hadn't quite figured out what he was going to say to her, but he knew he had to do it face-to-face. She deserved that much.

His mother glanced at Aaron, then focused her full attention back on Ant. "In a moment. But, sweetie, could you sit down for a second? There's something we need to talk about."

Ant eyed her as he sank into the same seat he'd stormed away from earlier. "If this is about me liking a girl, then—"

"No, it's not that." His mother fiddled with her fork. "Remember I told you that back in the day, your father moved out for two years? It wasn't just the drinking that made me ask him to leave." She looked up at the ceiling.

"Lord, he's never going to forgive me," she mumbled.

"Ma, Ant's not a kid anymore," Aaron said. "No more secrets, okay?"

Part of Ant wanted to yell, *No, no, no! I don't want to know! It's okay. I'll stay a little kid if you keep quiet.*

But Ant remained in place, mouth closed, and waited.

"When you were just a little thing, he got an invitation to play in a big poker tournament in one of the casinos in North Carolina. He didn't have a car—I'd already taken that from him, with all the drinking he was doing—so he was planning to catch a ride with Jasper. That morning, Aaron and I had stepped out to buy groceries. But while we were gone, Jasper stopped by. He wanted to leave early, probably to see some floozie." She took a deep breath. "So your father left a note on the table and rode off with him."

"And you're mad because he didn't tell you beforehand?" Ant asked.

She shook her head. "He was supposed to be watching you, Ant. He fed you, changed your diaper, put you in the crib, and left you. Alone."

His momma's words were heavy like concrete bricks tied to his ankles. Her eyes glistened with tears that were threatening to spill over. However, Ant didn't feel anything. Not hurt. Not sadness. Not even anger.

He was just numb.

"You were twenty months old. Aaron and I came home to find you sitting on the floor by your crib, bawling your eyes out. You had climbed out for the first time. Nothing happened, thank God. We were lucky. You could have hit your head. Or put something dangerous in your mouth. Or someone could have broken in and—" She caught herself before saying more. "And I knew, I *knew,* I couldn't live with a man who cared about drinking and gambling more than his own child. So I kicked him out. And it took me two years to give him another chance." She sighed. "I'll be honest—I don't know if I'm strong enough to go through that again. I don't know if I even want to try. And I know that's not what you want to hear, but you need to know the truth."

Aaron leaned in close to his brother. "You okay?"

Ant nodded his head so hard, he felt like his brain was bashing against his skull. "That's it?" He shrugged. "I thought y'all were going to say that he hit me or something."

"It's a big deal," Aaron said. "He broke our trust. And he broke the law. He should have gone to jail."

Ant stood up so fast that the chair almost tumbled over. "I know it was scary for y'all, but nothing happened.

I'm fine." He cracked a smile, then pulled out his phone. "So can I go to Shirley's place? She's expecting me."

Yolanda and Aaron looked at each other. Then his mother nodded. "Okay. But don't stay too long."

"Sure thing. Thanks, Ma."

Ant scurried out the door and bounced down the steps before she could change her mind.

But he didn't make it ten feet before his legs got all rubbery. And his eyes got watery. And all the hurt and lies and pain and anger caught up to him. Those cement blocks? They dragged him down. Way down. The weight of it was so heavy that he had to stop right on the sidewalk. He sank to the ground and drew his knees to his chest, squeezing himself as hard as he could.

He needed to breathe, but his lungs didn't seem to want to do their job. He pleaded with them to pull in air and push it back out. It felt like they wouldn't do it on their own if he didn't focus.

His father—the person he looked up to the most in the world—had abandoned him.

What type of man did that?

Maybe his mom was right. Maybe Ant's dad *didn't* deserve another chance.

# CHAPTER 45

My man sat there on that dirty sidewalk for at least ten minutes, doing his best to piece himself together. Honestly, I was afraid that he might stay there for hours on end, feeling all sorry for himself, and return home without talking to Shirley. And that wouldn't have done anybody any good.

Youngblood needed his partner, whether he knew it or not.

Ant finally stirred when he heard the rumble of thunder. A few gray clouds loomed overhead, blocking the afternoon sun.

He'd thought all the bad weather had passed. It hadn't rained in a week.

What can I say? Weather sure can be finicky.

The *last* thing Ant needed right then was to get caught

in another rainstorm, so he hightailed it down the street, only slowing once Shirley's house was in sight. She sat on her front steps, her legs stretched out into forever. He was surprised that she was sitting outside when it was about to pour, but when he looked up, all those ominous rain clouds had magically disappeared.

"Ant!" she called as he walked up the driveway. "I was wondering what happened . . ." She noticed the look on his face, then scampered to her feet. "Are you okay?"

He checked the mysterious weather once more, then asked, "Can we circle the block? I feel like I need to move."

She nodded, and they walked to the sidewalk.

Now that the clouds were gone, Ant could see his and Shirley's shadows bouncing along the ground ahead of them. They were so close, they almost looked like they were touching.

"So I guess I'll start," Shirley said. "I think you came over here to tell me that you don't want to be partners anymore. That true?"

"What makes you say that?" Ant asked, stretching out the inevitable.

"The way you sounded on the phone today. The way you acted on Monday when we were arguing. How weird you've been acting all week." She kicked at a rock with the tip of her sneaker. "Also, you didn't answer my question."

Ant watched the rock skip ahead of them. "I need to play with my brother," he finally said.

Shirley exhaled. "You were supposed to lead with three nice things."

"Sorry! I—"

"It was a joke, Ant."

"Oh."

"To be fair, it was a bad joke."

As they turned the corner, their shadows disappeared, blending into the street.

Then Shirley blew out a big breath. "Just be honest. Do you not want to play with me anymore because the boys are teasing you?"

Ant shook his head. "No!"

"It's okay," she continued. "I mean, it would be kind of horrible, but I get it."

If Ant had been braver, he would have reached out and offered her his hand. But instead, he said, "I promise. That's not it at all. I didn't even know you knew about that."

"Duh. You don't think I hear the whispers? The jokes?" Shirley fidgeted with one of her twists. "Does it bother you?"

Ant didn't hesitate. "Nope."

"Then why do you want to play with someone else? Your brother's a better player, right? You want to win that badly?"

Ant wished there was a rock on the sidewalk for *him* to kick.

"It's because of my dad," Ant said. "He's got a little drinking problem." He stopped walking. "Actually, he's an alcoholic."

Shirley froze in place.

"He's addicted to gambling, too. When I was younger, he . . ." The words caught in Ant's throat. He couldn't admit what his father had done. Not yet. "Mom kicked him out on Friday. I hadn't talked to him until today. And when he found out my brother was home, he assumed it was because Aaron was playing in the tournament. He sounded *so* happy. So I . . ."

"So you told him that y'all were partners?"

"Yeah," Ant said. "Dad promised he'd be there, and he promised not to drink."

They started walking again. After they turned left, Shirley asked, "Do you believe him?"

"I want to. But . . ." He thought back to the look on his mom's face when she'd told Ant about what'd happened when he was a baby. "Do you think we're supposed to help people we love, even if they hurt us?" Then he quickly added, "I mean, my dad didn't *hurt* me. He just . . . lied. About big things."

"I don't know, Ant. I guess it depends on the lie. On how much someone hurts you."

Ant shot Shirley a sideways glance. "Can I tell you something? Something serious. And you won't . . . I don't know, like, you won't feel sorry for me?" He didn't want to look *weak* in front of her. Anyone but her.

Shirley gave him a small, encouraging smile. "Of course."

Ant stared at the ground—that was much easier than looking at her. "This isn't the first time that my dad's drinking split up our family. He did it a lot when I was a kid. That, and the gambling. And even though I didn't know it, he always chose those things over us. Over me. And once he even—" Ant's voice broke, but he kept pushing through. "He left me at home, by myself, to go to a casino. I was a baby. My mom was out, and he just left me all alone."

After a few seconds, Ant took a chance and squinted in Shirley's direction. Now *she* was staring at the ground, her hands balled into fists.

"I lied," she said, her eyes glossy. "I'm *so* sorry that

happened to you. I can't believe he did that. That had to be scary."

As Shirley's eyes got all teary, Ant realized that she didn't think he was weak. She *cared* about him.

It was so surprising, it actually made Ant grin.

"What?" she asked as she wiped her eyes. "Can't I worry about my friend?"

"Sorry. I'm glad you care. I really do," Ant said. "The good thing is, I was little, so I don't remember it. My mom and Aaron do, though. That makes it hard for them to forgive my dad."

"I don't blame them," she said. "But *you* want to forgive him, don't you?"

Ant shrugged. "I'm mad . . . but he's still my dad. I want him to be okay. To get better and come home."

Shirley reached out like she was going to put her hand on Ant's shoulder, but she pulled her arm back before making contact. "You really are one of the kindest people I know."

"Yeah. And water is wet."

They both laughed. Then Shirley's expression grew serious again.

"My dad—that is, my biological father—was kind of like yours. But worse. He *did* hurt us, in the bad way."

Ant sucked in a sharp breath. "Oh, Shirley, I—"

"Nope! No sympathy needed," she said as she kept marching forward.

"Why is it okay for you and not for me?"

"I don't know! I'll ask my therapist the next time I talk to her. Anyway, all I was going to say was that I understand how you can love someone but still not trust them." They turned the corner. "Also, I think you and your brother should play together."

"Really?"

"You're trying to save your dad. How can I get in the way of that?" She tugged at another twist. "Although, my parents were really excited about watching us."

"I'm sorry. Maybe Bobby can step in."

"He's too young. Plus, the deadline to enter already passed."

"Oh yeah. But maybe Mr. Eugene can—"

"Ant. It's okay."

Ant stuffed his hands into his pockets. "If we win, do you want my share of the prize money? That only seems fair."

"I don't care about that."

"Then why did you agree to play with me?"

She didn't reply.

They reached the end of the block and turned back

onto Shirley's street. Ant could see their shadows again, almost touching. And Shirley still hadn't answered him.

"I'm sorry the boys at school have been teasing you," she finally said.

"It's okay. Have Rochelle and Layla and all them been teasing you?"

She gave a half-hearted laugh. "Only my mom."

"I'm pretty sure you won't have to worry about that once you tell her I bailed on you."

"Don't worry. I won't tell my parents about your father," she said. "I'm guessing you want me to keep it a secret."

Ant thought about that as they ambled their way back to her house. Maybe that was the problem—people keeping too many secrets.

"See you tomorrow?" he asked.

"Of course." Shirley started to climb the steps, then turned around. "Ant, I'm really sorry about your dad. But I think you're doing the right thing. I would do the same."

"Thanks."

"I hope it all works out."

"Me too."

"And thank you for trusting me. I know talking about that kind of stuff is hard."

"Same," Ant said. "Thanks for telling me about your biological dad. He sounds horrible."

"He was." She hopped up the rest of the steps to her door. "Hey—I'll be around later, if you want to talk. About spades or your dad . . . or anything."

"I'm not a horse."

"That's my line."

"And water is wet."

"Now you're just—"

"We're quite a rotten pair. Or is it pear?"

"Boy, bye!" she yelled as she stepped into the house.

Youngblood started the long walk home, with maybe a little more strut in his stride, but something made him look back at the house. Or someone.

And this time, there was no mistaking who was in the window, staring back.

# CHAPTER 46

"What do you mean, you need a new partner?"

"Come on, Aaron," Ant pleaded on Friday morning. "Shirley had to drop out. You've *got* to play with me!"

Ant had neglected to mention that he'd been the one to ask Shirley to bow out, not the other way around. But Aaron didn't need to know that.

"Plus, once Dad is better, we can tell him all about how we won the tournament as a team," Ant said.

He'd also glossed over the fact that their father planned to come to the tournament to see his sons in action. That boy had been practicing his bluffing skills a lot lately.

*Minor details,* Ant told himself.

"You know you miss playing spades." Ant sat down beside his brother on the edge of Aaron's bed. It wasn't lost on Ant that he'd been sitting in the same spot last week, talking to his father. "It'll be fun."

"I guess," Aaron said. "Ma could use the distraction."

"See! Perfect!"

"You're sure Shirley is okay with this?"

"Yeah." Ant smiled. "She wasn't all that interested in winning the prize money anyway."

Aaron arched an eyebrow. "What does that look mean?"

Ant stopped smiling. "What look?"

"Forget it," his brother said. "I've learned my lesson about teasing you. And speaking of lessons learned . . ." He took a deep breath. "Dad's not going to magically change just because we win some tournament."

"We have to do something," Ant said. "Make him see what he's going to miss if he keeps at it. Besides, he deserves another chance."

Aaron stood up. "He's had at least two chances, Ant. Probably more. How many more times do you want him to hurt our family? To hurt Ma?"

Ant stared at a basketball poster on the wall behind Aaron so he wouldn't have to focus on his brother's eyes. "I don't understand. Why doesn't he want to get help?"

"For the same reason he got so mad when Ma started

working those early shifts at the emergency clinic. Dad doesn't want to look weak."

"I hate that word. *Weak*."

"Yeah, me too." Aaron began pacing the room. "Dad acts like it's okay for other people to be weak—to be vulnerable—but not him. Take my flute. Some people would say that it's the least macho instrument a man can play. It's *weak* with a megasized *W*. But Dad never gave me grief over it. If anything, it was his encouragement that kept me going, even when kids teased me so much that I wanted to quit."

"Lucky you," Ant said. "He never did that for me."

"What are you talking about?"

"The spades tournament. The way he always talks about it. Like it's this big Joplin family tradition. And when things went the way they did last year, he acted like . . . like he was ashamed of me. Like he didn't think I was tough enough to play."

"Oh, Ant. I'm sorry. Dad has this old-school notion that you have to be tough to make it in the world. But he's wrong. There's nothing wrong with showing emotion. Or admitting when you're in over your head. Or even asking for help." Aaron rubbed the back of his neck. "Are you sure about the tournament? Teenagers are vicious. They won't take it easy on you, especially if we're winning."

Ant glanced at the spot on the bedspread where his father had spilled his drink. It had almost faded, but Ant could still make out the edges of the stain.

He wasn't sure if he was ready, but he didn't have a choice. My man knew that sometimes, you gotta go with your gut. And his gut was telling him to stay the course. If a youngblood like Ant could stand tall and show the world what he was made of—win or lose—maybe his daddy would be inclined to do the same. And if there was any chance of that happening, Ant had to try. After all, you lose one hundred percent of the games you're too scared to play.

"That day . . . when Dad left you alone," Aaron said after a moment. "I was the one who found you."

Ant watched his brother's head sink into his hands.

"I ran inside to ask Dad to help Ma unload the groceries. I still remember seeing you crawling around your room, looking for someone to pick you up. Maybe that's why I can't help calling you little—'cause I always see you like that." Aaron sank onto the bed next to his brother. "I don't know if Ma can go through that again. Shoot, I don't know if *I* can. I had nightmares for, like, three months afterward."

Ant tried to imagine how it would feel if he was the older brother. The one who'd seen his dad at his worst.

Aaron gulped. "Sometimes I think it's all *my* fault."

"Why?"

"I should have stayed home that day. I know how long it takes Ma to shop. And how reckless Dad was back then. I could have stopped him from leaving. Or at least stayed with you, so you wouldn't have been alone."

Ant nudged his brother, trying to lighten the mood. "It's not your fault."

"Yeah. Just like it's not yours."

Ant tapped his chest, right over his heart. "Does that guilty feeling ever go away?"

"I'll let you know once I find out." Aaron tapped his chest as well. "Even though I'm home under crummy circumstances, I'm happy to be playing with you."

"Me too. But if we're going to be partners, I have one rule," Ant said. "So about trash talking . . ."

On the walk to school, Ant texted his father, just to make sure he was okay. To make sure that he was still sober.

His father replied quickly, telling Ant not to worry, that he was "back on the straight and narrow" and that nothing could keep him away from seeing his boys.

Then Roland texted a picture of himself, all smiles.

Kinda like a crocodile.

Something about that smile made Ant nervous like it never had before.

As he switched his phone off and slipped it into his backpack, Shirley waved him over. He'd been worried that now that she'd had time to think about it, she'd be mad at him for dumping her. But she wasn't. In fact, she was bursting to tell him that, while she hadn't outright lied to her parents, she'd led them to believe that it was *her* choice not to play in the tournament. Kinda like what Ant had done to Aaron. She even promised to go to the tournament with the Joplins to cheer them on.

Youngblood had really hit the jackpot when it came to his friends.

Or at least, *some* of his friends.

Later that morning, when Ant left the room to get a sip of water, Jamal followed him out the door.

"I heard that you and Aaron are playing in the tournament together," Jamal said, catching up to him. "Y'all better not cheat."

Ant stopped walking. "What makes you think we'd do something like that?"

"Well, how else did your brother win all those games?"

"Um . . . he was good?"

"That's not what Taj says." Jamal smirked. "Actually, Taj just told me some other stuff about your family."

Ant tensed. "What does that mean?"

Jamal stepped closer to Ant. "Just saying, you and your family have *always* looked down on us. Like how you and your mom were trying to give me a handout last week."

Ant frowned. The only thing he remembered was his mother asking Jamal to stay over for dinner.

"So how does it feel now that the shoe's on the other foot?" Jamal asked. "Not so cool when everyone is gossiping behind *your* back, huh?"

"Jamal, I . . ." Ant stalled out as Terrence popped his head outside of the door.

"Are y'all almost finished?" Terrence asked. "I want to get some water, too."

"Yeah. We're done," Jamal said as he walked back to the classroom. "See you tomorrow, little Ant."

# CHAPTER 47

On Saturday morning, the park was already starting to fill up by the time Ant and his crew arrived. Vendors from all over the city had filled their booths with everything from West African dashikis and handmade jewelry to pork ribs and chicken bog—that means chicken and rice, for you young'uns that don't know better. Kids played a pickup game on one basketball court while large speakers and a portable stage were being set up on another. The Spectacular Branch Brothers, a local gospel group made up of guys so old that their wrinkles had wrinkles, always closed out the festival. Ant didn't necessarily like all those ancient church songs, but even *his* foot got to a-tapping and his head got to a-bobbing when those old fellas started singing and strutting across the stage.

Ant also loved watching Shirley take it all in, and hated the idea of it going away next year.

His momma wore a green summer dress—way fancier than the T-shirt and jeans she usually wore on the weekends. She had even dabbed on a little lipstick to go along with her grin. Ant was happy to see her all spiffy-looking, especially given how down she'd been all week.

They slowly worked their way through the booths. Aaron tried to grab a free sample of that chicken bog, but Ant elbowed him on. As good as all the food smelled, he wanted to power ahead to the pavilion in the center of the park where the tournament would be taking place. But his mother kept lingering at each and every booth. She even stopped to chat with a vendor selling long wooden earrings, despite the fact that her ears weren't pierced.

"Ma," Ant finally said. "We really need to check in."

"Why don't y'all go ahead," she said. "Shirley, you mind keeping me company?"

"Sure." Shirley waved goodbye to Ant, and followed his mother in the opposite direction, toward a woman selling blackberry-scented Epsom salts.

"Ma's really nervous," Aaron said as they started off. "I'm pretty sure she thinks that Dad might show up."

Ant almost tripped. "Would that be a bad thing?"

"Probably."

"Why? Because she doesn't want to see him?"

"They've been married for twenty years. Of course she wants to see him. She's just scared that he'll pop up drunk and make a scene." He shrugged. "What? You think she got all dressed up for *you*?"

Ant looked back at his mom and her green dress. It was his *father's* favorite.

Then he stole a quick glance at his phone. Ant had texted his father that morning to make sure that he was still coming, but hadn't heard back yet.

As they neared the pavilion, Ant took in the sea of mismatched card tables. This was an "if you got it, bring it" type of event. The tables, playing cards, and even pens and pads had all been loaned out for the day. In the corner of the pavilion sat Mr. Eugene, along with the rest of the old-timers from the store.

"And here come the famous Joplin boys," Mr. Eugene said, flipping a page in his notebook. "Ant, where's your partner?"

"Actually, we need to make a switch," Ant said. "Aaron is taking Shirley's place."

"Oh, that's too bad," Mr. Casey said. "I was looking forward to seeing the firecracker play."

He wasn't the only one.

"Well, y'all are at table five," Mr. Eugene said. "Brought cards?"

"Sure did," Aaron said. "How many teams are there?"

"Sixteen. Came out of the woodwork when they heard I'd increased the pot, all of them hoping for a quick payday." He looked squarely at Ant. "This is way different than the younger tournament, slick. I don't know some of these kids—don't know how they were raised. And the ones I do know have grown a lot, both in size and lip. Especially that one."

They turned to see Taj and Jamal walking toward the registration table. Taj hadn't seen them yet, but Jamal had. Ant wasn't sure what to do to defuse the tension between them. He settled on a half-hearted head nod.

Jamal scowled, and nudged his brother while pointing at Ant. Taj looked up. Then he smirked.

"We got trouble," Ant whispered to his brother as Taj and Jamal started toward them. "Should we bounce?"

Ant thought that his brother would want to walk away, but Aaron remained in place. "Why?" he whispered back. "We haven't done anything wrong."

"Wassup, fellas," Taj said once they'd reached them. "Y'all ready for this beatdown?" Not waiting for a reply,

Taj turned to Aaron. "So you decided to leave that fancy school of yours to hang with us regular folks? Or are you just scared that your brother's going to buckle under the pressure like last year?"

Ant fought the temptation to remind Taj that it was Ant *and* Jamal who'd lost last year.

"Don't worry," Taj said. "We'll make this whippin' real quick so you can get back to your snobby new friends." He leaned closer. "You do still remember how to play, right? Or are you too busy playing that flute?" He started prancing around, playing an imaginary instrument. "Is that how you do it? I bet that's how the boys—oh, I mean the *girls*—like it."

If Aaron was bothered, he didn't show it. "It looks like you're pretending to play a piccolo, not a flute."

From the look on Taj's face, Ant realized that he had no clue what a piccolo was. But then Taj sneered. "I saw your pops at the Quick Mart the other day. The man was buying enough beer to last for a month."

Ant and Aaron both stiffened like too-thick cornbread batter.

"We can't talk now," Taj continued. "But don't worry. If we end up playing against each other, I'd be happy to describe how jacked-up your dad looked." He gave the

Joplins one last mocking glare, then pushed Jamal toward the registration table.

"Ignore Taj," Aaron said as he led Ant back into the festival marketplace. "He's trying to get into our heads. Throw us off our game."

"That was a low blow, bringing up Dad," Ant said.

Aaron paused to grab a sample of barbecue from a booth called the Whole Hog. "Just be ready. They're gonna sling a lot more mud, especially if we face them in the tournament."

"But doesn't all the stuff that Taj said bother you? You know, like boys liking you—"

"Why do I care if boys are interested in me?" Aaron wolfed down the rest of his sample. "What does that have to do with me? Who *I'm* interested in?"

Ant thought for a moment. "Nothing, I guess."

"Besides, only an idiot thinks it's weak to be gay." Aaron looked at his watch. "I'm still hungry. I'm going to grab a sandwich before the tournament. Want one?"

"No thanks. You go ahead," Ant said.

While Aaron got in line and scanned the menu, Ant stepped away and checked his phone again. There was still no message from his father, so he decided to call him.

"Hey? Ant?" his father answered.

"Dad! Where are you?"

"I'm sorry! I lost track of time. But I'm on my way now!"

Ant smiled. He knew his father would keep his promise. "So I'll see you in a few minutes. We'll be at the pavilion—"

"Actually, it'll probably be an hour or so," his dad interrupted. "I, uh, had to run out of town last night. We're just heading back now." There was some mumbling on the other end of the phone, but Ant couldn't make it out. "Alright, gotta go, son. See you soon."

"Wait. Dad—"

But he was gone.

Ant trudged back to the Whole Hog, where Aaron had already demolished half of his sandwich. "You okay?" Aaron asked. "Seriously, don't worry about Taj. It's all going to work out." He nodded toward the barbecue booth. "Come on, let me buy you a sandwich. Nobody likes to play cards on an empty stomach."

# CHAPTER 48

A couple of sandwiches later, Ant and Aaron settled down in their seats. Jamal and his brother sat a couple of tables down from them. The tables had been set up in a two-by-four grid, with people milling about, ready to see the action—and trash talk—up close. Ant hoped that once the first round started, his mom and Shirley would stand *behind* him—he was a smidge worried that he'd spend more time looking at Shirley than at Aaron.

A microphone squeaked, and everyone turned to see Mr. Eugene standing at the edge of the pavilion. "Welcome to the twenty-second annual Oak Grove Spades Tournament," he announced. "First, I want to thank our sponsors—namely, me."

Everyone laughed. Then Mr. Eugene went on to

thank a number of the people and businesses who had volunteered their money and time. Next he went over the rules, not that he needed to. They weren't nothing tricky, just the standard set. Plus, it wasn't like they ever changed.

"Now, for all you spectators out there, once the first round starts, that's exactly what you have to do. *Spectate.* That means no talking to the teams, no giving signals, nothing like that." He started toward his chair. "And while trash talk is allowed—maybe even encouraged—I don't want to hear any cursing. Got it?"

As everyone nodded, Ant took in the crowd. He recognized a bunch of faces—kids from church, his class, neighbors, and even Mrs. Booker.

Everyone was there.

Everyone except his dad.

"Alright," Mr. Eugene said. "Cell phones off, and let's get crackin'!"

The first two teams that Ant and Aaron played against—ThunderSauce and Beelzebub, Incorporated—well, let's be honest. They stank more than a bowl of three-day-old chitlins on a hot summer day. But neither team held it against the boys for losing so bad.

One of 'em even seemed relieved, because once they were bounced, they were free to run off across town to that video-game festival.

Ant's momma couldn't quite catch on to the "no talking" rule. Ant could hear every sigh, cheer, and question she whispered to Shirley. His mother was so loud, Ant swore that he could even hear her rolling her eyes.

Shirley must have noticed how this was affecting Ant, because after the first two rounds, she suggested that they move a little farther away to "give the boys their space." After all, she didn't want to throw the team off of their game.

That Shirley was a great partner—even when she wasn't sitting at the table.

In the third round, Ant and Aaron faced off against a team called TWINZZZ, because, well, they were twins. Aaron had played against them twice before.

"Since when did they let little kids into this tournament?" Malcolm Draper asked as Ant sat down. "Shouldn't you be playing with mud pies or something?"

"Yeah, ain't it time for your nap?" Bishop added. Bishop was a little shorter than Malcolm, with a few more freckles on his face.

"At least he knows how to spell. Y'all do know the

word *twins* doesn't have any Zs in it, right?" Aaron pointed to the deck. "High card gets first deal?"

Malcolm nodded. He cut the deck, then held it out to Aaron to choose a card.

Aaron pumped his fist—his jack of diamonds beat Malcolm's three of clubs.

And that's when their luck with the cards took a tumble.

Ant ended up with only two spades and seven clubs in his first hand, along with a bunch of trash cards. He'd be lucky to win two books.

He stole a glance at his brother. Aaron stared at his cards, his eyebrows furrowed. It was impossible to read his expression—one of the faults of being paired with a new partner. Over the past week, he'd gotten pretty good at reading Shirley's facial expressions. Or rather, the expressions she *wanted* him to understand.

That gave him an idea.

Ant spackled a cake-eating grin on his face and started moving his cards all around in his hand. Then, somehow *widening* his grin, he started counting to himself as he pointed to the cards.

*"One, two, three, four, five, six,"* he whispered.

He paused, then repeated it again, one through six.

And then just to top things off, he did a little shimmy in his seat. The boy was celebrating more than an overweight turkey the day *after* Thanksgiving.

He looked up to see Aaron frowning at him. But so were Malcolm and Bishop.

"Aaron, I think I have— Oh, my bad." Ant turned to Malcolm. "It's y'all's bid first, right?"

Malcolm squinted at Ant. "I feel pretty good about my hand. But it's better to be safe than sorry. I got four. No, make that three and a possible." He shook his head, then looked at Ant again.

Ant's grin expanded as he glanced at his hand and started counting all over again.

"Make that three," Malcolm said to his brother.

The twins—I mean, TWINZZZ—ended up with a bid of six books. As soon as Malcolm wrote the score down on the notepad, the smile disappeared from Ant's face.

"I got two," he said. "Maybe."

"What?" Aaron said. "But what about—"

And then, he *got* it.

Unfortunately for the TWINZZZ, they weren't as quick on the come up. "What do you mean, only two books?" Malcolm asked. "What was with all that dancing and smiling?"

"What? I was smiling?" Ant asked. "I didn't realize it. I guess I'm just happy to be here."

"That's cheating!" Bishop said.

"Since when is smiling cheating?" Ant asked.

"It's sending signals," Malcolm said.

"To who?" both Ant and Aaron said at the same time.

"You know what? I don't care," Bishop said. "We're still gonna get our six books. Or are you too young to count that high, little man?"

"Oh, you're gonna win lot more than that," Ant said. "But you're only going to get *credit* for six books—remember, no points for sandbags. So we'll get our four—"

"And you'll only be up by twenty points," Aaron said. "But maybe you'd better check our math, just to be sure. Or do you want me to draw you a picture? I know big words like *four* are hard for you."

Ant glared at his brother. "Remember what I said about trash talk?"

"That wasn't trash talk. I was just pontificating on the intersection of math and arts education." He turned to Malcolm and snapped his fingers. "You heard the man. Put us down for four books, and let's play."

# CHAPTER 49

Sure enough, Ant and Aaron won four books—scoring forty points—to the TWINZZZ's nine books—and only sixty points—in that first hand. But wouldn't you know it, in the next hand, it was the Antagonists' turn to win nine books. Of course, they were also smart enough to *bid* nine, and collect those ninety points.

Two hands later, Ant and Aaron had made it to the finals.

"Nice playing," Malcolm said to Ant, giving him some dap. "You're alright, for a little kid."

Ant could have corrected him, but winning seemed to make everything sting a lot less.

"How does it feel, being in the finals?" Aaron asked as they rose from the table.

"Good. I thought it would be harder."

"We've been really lucky with the cards—plus those first two teams were awful." Aaron nodded toward their cheering section. "I'm glad Shirley is here. Ma would have been a nervous wreck without her, probably peeking over her shoulder every chance she got, hoping for Dad."

Ant had been so focused on the games, *he* hadn't even thought about his father.

He switched on his phone, but before he could check it, his mom and Shirley rushed over to congratulate them.

"Y'all did great!" his mom said. "You're in the finals!"

"Thanks, Ma," Aaron said. "I mean . . . it's not like I've never been there before."

"Don't get cocky, Aaron."

Ant was still staring at his phone when Shirley nudged him. "You okay?"

"Oh. Just waiting for my phone to power up," he said. "Thanks for staying here with Ma."

"Are you kidding? She's so cool!"

"Are we talking about the same woman?" Ant asked.

"I like the way you outsmarted that other team during your first bid," Shirley said. "Misdirection for the win. That's what those guys get for underestimating you!"

"Thanks. What about Jamal and Taj? How are they doing?"

"They just started a new hand," she said. "Unless they totally bomb—which I doubt—they're going to make it to the finals."

"Ugh. I was hoping we wouldn't have to face them. They're going to come at us about my dad."

"You're probably right," she said. "Plus, I think they're cheating."

"Of course they are," Ant said. "I can't believe Jamal would be so—"

Ant froze. His phone had finally come to life.

"Ant?"

"Um . . ." He stepped away from Aaron and his mom, and motioned for Shirley to follow him. "My dad is here."

"Great! I mean, that *is* great, right?"

"He said he's . . ." Ant paused to read the message again, hoping he'd misunderstood it. "He said that he's hanging out with Mr. Gramm."

"Mr. Gramm?" She frowned. "Isn't that the old guy who's always . . . ?"

"Drunk." Ant stole a glance at his mom and her fancy dress. "I have to find him. Before I tell Ma that he's here, I need to see if he's . . . I need to know—"

“I understand,” she said. “What do you want me to do?”

“Just have your phone ready, in case I need to text you, he said. “Mr. Eugene always takes a ten-minute break between the last round and the finals. I should be back by then.”

“You don’t want me to come along?”

“Better not.” It would be bad enough if his dad was a mess. He didn’t think he could take it if Shirley saw that firsthand.

“Okay.” She gave him a nervous smile that somehow still reassured him. “Good luck, Ant.”

Ant slipped out of the pavilion, but he wasn’t sure where to look first. He spun around, scanning the crowd for his father’s telltale grin. When he didn’t spot it, he decided to start with the benches near the basketball courts. But a lot more people had packed into the park since the tournament started. And Ant wasn’t exactly the tallest fella out there, which made it hard for him to see.

He wandered along the winding concrete paths, passing the basketball courts, the tennis courts, and the playground, all while keeping an eye out for his father or Mr. Gramm’s porkpie hat. But either his father was walking around just as much as Ant was, or he wasn’t there after all.

Ant reached the edge of the park, unsure where to search next. Then he heard a familiar cackle. He followed it through the park gate and around the corner. Sure enough, there was Roland Joplin, leaning against a pickup truck, along with Mr. Gramm and two other men.

His father held a red plastic cup in his hand. He took a swig from it, and held it out to Mr. Gramm, who refilled it with whatever was hidden in his brown paper bag. Then his dad laughed at something so hard that his drink sloshed out of the cup. But that just made Roland sloppily motion for Mr. Gramm to pour more back in.

His dad's voice rang out as he said, "Now pay attention. This is how *real* men drink."

And then he downed the cup.

As Mr. Gramm and the other drunks cracked up along with his father, Ant felt his heart shattering into a thousand tiny splinters.

And way, way up in that grandstand in the sky, my heart shattered right with along with youngblood's, piece by jagged piece.

# CHAPTER 50

Ant wanted to turn around and run in the opposite direction. To pretend that he'd never seen anything. To slip back into the crowd, find a quiet spot where no one could find him, and hide.

But he knew his daddy would eventually make his way over to the pavilion. Ant's momma, with her fancy dress and pretty smile, would be crushed. And any chance of putting the broken pieces of his family back together would disappear.

Ant knew he had to confront his father.

But as I've been saying all along, the boy wasn't no dummy. He knew he couldn't do it on his own. He needed help.

So Ant pulled out his phone and typed a text to Shirley.

"Ant! That you?"

Ant looked up. His father squinted hard at him, before he broke into a grin. Then he quickly handed the cup off to one of his friends. "That sure is you! I was about to head your way!"

Ant pocketed his phone as his father sauntered over. Roland's shadow zigged and zagged with every step he took. Then his father eclipsed Ant as he enveloped him in a giant bear hug. The black-and-gray prickles along his father's unshaven face scratched at Ant's cheek.

Ant recognized the musty, sweaty odor he'd smelled on Mr. Gramm last week. But now the scent clung to his father—accompanied by stale breath and bloodshot eyes.

"See! I told you I'd be here," his father said with a forced laugh.

"Dad," Ant said. "You promised. You said that you weren't drinking anymore."

"What? You mean that cup?" He thumbed toward the truck. "I was just holding it—*pretending.* You know how those fellas can be. They'll harass you to death unless you at least *look* like you're drinking. They'll think you're strange otherwise."

*You mean they'll think you're weak.*

"So is everyone over at the pavilion?" His father rubbed his hands together. "Aaron and your momma? I can't wait to see 'em!"

"Dad. I can *smell* it on you."

Roland's eyes sparkled as he turned on the charm. "Anthony. Come on."

"No, Dad." Ant balled up his fists, his muscles tense and jittery. "You're an alcoholic."

His father stopped smiling. "Watch your tone, boy."

"That's the problem with these children nowadays," Mr. Gramm heckled as he waved a cup in the air. "Always talking back to their elders. Don't know when they're supposed to keep their mouths shut."

Roland glanced at Mr. Gramm, then turned to Ant. "Look, son, that's enough backtalk. You need to remember who you're speaking to." He put his hand on Ant's shoulder. "Why don't you calm down—"

"You are an alcoholic and a liar!" Ant said, shrugging him off. "Where were you this morning? Gambling with more of Aaron's tuition money?"

"You know, I am sick and tired of all y'all telling me how I can or can't make money," he said. "Yeah, I was playing cards. Won over five hundred dollars. So why don't you and everyone else get off your high horse! That is, unless you don't want what this money buys."

"We don't care about the money."

"I bet your momma would say otherwise." He scrubbed his hands over his face. "You're a smart kid, Anthony. Use that brain of yours." He held out his arms, like he was putting himself on display. "Just because I've been drinking doesn't mean that I'm a drunk. Come on, do I look drunk?"

Then the fool actually spun around in place.

Like a drunk.

"I'll be back in a little bit," Roland called to his compatriots. "I gotta see my boys play in the tournament." He motioned to Ant. "Come on, son. Get those little legs pumping."

Ant didn't know what was taking Aaron so long, but he couldn't let his father get to that pavilion. So he took a deep breath, straightened himself up nice and tall, and said, "You were in North Carolina, right? At the casino?" He paused, then added, "Like last time?"

His father frowned. "What does that mean?"

"Ma told me what happened when I was a baby," Ant said, the words fast and slippery on his tongue. "How you . . . *abandoned* me."

For a moment, time seemed to stop. Everything went silent, even the birds and the squirrels.

Then Roland's face transformed into something angry and evil, like the Wolf Man from an old horror movie. The way he *snarled* at his son? It was unlike anything I had ever seen.

It was the stuff nightmares were made of.

"She *told* you?" He hocked a wad of spit onto the ground. "She promised me. *Promised!*"

"I'm old enough to know the truth. Ma thought it would help me understand—"

"Your mother didn't have the right to tell you that." He wiped his nose, which was starting to run. "See, the fellas told me this is what happens when the woman has too much power in a relationship. Just because she makes a little more money than me—"

"Dad!"

"I should have known better. She's trying to turn my own kids against me. First Aaron, and now you. *He* won't even return my calls. Wants to 'have your momma's back,' whatever that means." Roland started toward the park. "She and I need to have a face-to-face. Now."

Ant didn't know what to do. This wasn't part of his plan.

He was only ten. Old enough for some things, but not for dealing with his daddy's rage on his own.

But he knew he had to do *something,* so he scampered in front of his father, blocking his path. His shadow seemed so small compared to Roland's. "No, Dad," Ant said. "You're not going. I won't allow it."

His father took a step back. "You won't *allow* it? Who do you think you are?" He cut to the left, trying to get around Ant. But he didn't see the rock on the edge of the sidewalk. His foot slipped, and he went tumbling to the ground, smashing his face against the cement.

That rock wasn't much more than a pebble. But even the littlest things sure can be pesky. They pop up when you least expect them. And sometimes they can topple giants.

Roland sat up, a trail of blood oozing from his nose, which now looked crooked.

"What's going on here?"

Ant turned to find Aaron rushing toward him, with Shirley a few steps behind. Ant had never been more relieved in his life. Neither had I.

"Are you alright?" Aaron asked his brother. "You're shaking."

"I'm fine. It's just . . ." Ant stuffed his hands in his pockets. "Dad's . . . I don't know what to do."

"Don't worry. I'll take it from here." Aaron looked at his father. "Are you okay, Dad?" he asked through clenched teeth.

"Aaron," his father started. Then his shoulders deflated. "Boys. I . . ."

The mighty Roland Joplin, with his wrinkled clothes and bleeding face, was nothing like the man he claimed to be. The man he'd been raised to be. And as Ant and Aaron looked at him, they saw something in their father's eyes that they'd never seen before.

Roland wasn't going to cry. There were no tears there, waiting to spill out. It was more that his eyes were too sad for crying. Like they'd already squeezed out every drop they could. And his shoulders hung so low, his arms might as well have been made of lead.

Ant could tell Aaron wanted to hit him. Maybe he *should* have hit him. But instead, he helped their father to his feet. "Let's go, Dad. I'll take you to a hospital."

"You can't," his father said, trying to pulling away from Aaron. "What about the tournament? If you leave, your brother can't—"

"I know, Dad," Ant said. "It's okay."

Aaron seemed to hesitate. "You sure?"

"Yeah," Ant said. "Go on and take him to the hospital."

Aaron nodded. His grip was firm on his father's arm. "Did you drive here?"

His father remained silent.

"You *did*, didn't you? I can't believe . . ." Aaron started dragging him away. "Come on. And give me your keys."

They were halfway down the sidewalk when Roland turned back to Ant. "I love you, son."

After a moment, Ant replied, "I love you, too."

Because even after everything that had happened, he believed his father's words.

Just as much as he believed his own.

# CHAPTER 51

Ant made his way back to the park. He spotted an empty bench. The crying began before he even sat down.

He felt drained.

Exhausted.

Alone.

But my man *wasn't* alone. Shirley plopped down next to him. She didn't say anything at first. She just opened up her hand, palm up. An invitation.

Ant slipped his hand into hers. Pecan tan against mahogany brown.

Shirley took a deep breath. "I know you probably didn't want me to see that, but I—"

"Thank you," Ant interrupted, not bothering to wipe the

tears from his face. "I'm glad you're here, even though that was really embarrassing."

She squeezed his hand. "Ant, *he* was embarrassing. You were *brave*."

He didn't feel brave. But if it meant that Shirley kept holding his hand like that, he'd take it.

"Maybe we should go tell your mom what happened," she continued. "I left her with Mrs. Booker."

"I don't even know what to say to her. How do I explain all . . . *this*?"

"Don't worry." She squeezed his hand again. "We'll figure something out."

Ant paused for a moment. Shirley really was a great partner. "I'm sorry for asking you to drop out of the tournament," he said. "I shouldn't have done that."

"Yeah, and water is wet."

He looked up. "Seriously. I like playing with you way more than with Aaron." Ant gulped. "Like, way, way, *way* more."

Shirley smiled.

Ant smiled back.

Then . . . his phone buzzed with a text.

And I promise, I had *nothing* to do with it!

Ant reluctantly let go of her hand so he could pull the phone from his pocket. "It's Ma," he said. "They're about to start the final round." He began to put his phone away, but stopped and squinted at the screen. Then he frowned.

"Something wrong?" Shirley asked.

"I wrote you a text, telling you about Dad. But . . . I never sent it." He shrugged. "I guess I was really lucky that you and Aaron decided to come find me."

A clouded expression came to Shirley's face. "Yeah. Lucky."

Ant sat up. "I feel like there's something you're hiding."

"It's . . . forget it."

"Come on," he said, nudging her. "What is it? You know you can tell me anything."

She gave him a sideways glance. "Okay, but don't laugh."

"Deal."

She sighed. "I heard a voice. It was like someone was whispering to me, but when I turned around, no one was there."

Ant tried his best to hold the giggle in but failed.

She made a fist. "Ant!"

"Okay, okay," he said. "I'm sorry. What did the voice say?"

"It said . . ." She pointed at him. "For real, promise that you won't laugh."

Ant crossed his heart. "Promise."

"The voice said, *'Go find your partner. Youngblood needs you.'* And then it told me where to look."

Ant cocked his head. *"Youngblood?"*

"Don't laugh!"

"I'm not," Ant said. "It's just—I haven't heard that word since my granddad died. It's what he always called me and Aaron."

Now, I know what you're wondering. Is this for real? But come on—who did you *think* was narrating this story?

"Are you playing with me?" Ant asked. "Seriously?"

"I'm not! But who knows—maybe it's a sign," Shirley said. "Maybe *we're* supposed to be partners for the finals."

"Against Taj and Jamal?" Ant groaned. "They're gonna talk so much trash."

Shirley rolled her eyes. "Ant, you just faced down your father. If you can do that, I'm sure you can stand a little trash talk."

He had to admit, Shirley had a point. Compared to Roland, Taj and Jamal were like a package of unsalted soda crackers. Tasteless, sure, but also harmless.

"You're right. And I bet Mr. Eugene will let the Antagonists make a substitution, this being an emergency situation and all." Ant stood up. "Ready?"

Shirley nodded and jumped to her feet.

They didn't speak for the first minute or so, and for a moment, youngblood worried that something was wrong. Maybe she was still thinking about the mysterious—and *captivating*—voice that had led her to him.

Or perhaps she was stewing over something else. Like how they had just been holding hands.

Maybe he wasn't supposed to let go of her hand when they were sitting on the bench. Maybe she wanted to hold his hand *all* the time.

And maybe—gulp—she wanted even more than that.

But also, Ant wasn't about to run away from this problem.

"Everything alright?" he asked her.

"Um, yeah," she said. "I was just looking at our shadows."

Sure enough, their shadows bounced on the sidewalk ahead of them, hers stretched out a little farther than his.

They looked like they were holding hands.

Ant's cheeks heated. But inside he was feeling like the tallest, bravest fella in that park. "You know I like you, right?" he said.

"Duh. Of course you do. I'm fabulous."

Ant waited for a few seconds. When she didn't elaborate, he faked a cough under his breath.

"Oh yeah. I like you, too," Shirley admitted. Then she lightly punched his shoulder. "Come on, I'll race you! Winner buys the other ice cream?"

The pair of them took off toward the pavilion like two squirrels chasing after a truckload of walnuts.

There'd be plenty of time to hold hands later on.

Right now, they had a game to play.

# CHAPTER 52

Now you're probably wondering how the finals went. I bet you're imagining that the championship game was a long, hard-fought battle. That each team tried to outbid their opponents, setting each other over and over as the crowd hooted and hollered around them.

But the fact of the matter was, Ant and Shirley beat Taj and Jamal like a dirty carpet. Drummed them like a snare in a marching band. Whipped them like a fancy fondue.

Shucks—they won by so much, Taj and Jamal didn't even stick around for the final cards to be played.

And sure, Taj and his brother talked a little trash. Even mentioned Ant's father. And that hurt because Ant knew being Jamal's friend was going to be mighty difficult after something like that. But like Shirley said, there was nothing those boys could do that would be harder for Ant to deal with than standing up to Roland had been.

Speaking of Roland—my boy—he had a battle to wage as well. And it wasn't one that would end once he reached two hundred points. Roland was an alcoholic and a gambling addict. He was going to have to live with—and fight against—those addictions for the rest of his life.

On that Saturday he saw shame and disappointment reflected in his sons' eyes. Saw what he was giving up. And what strength really looked like. So once he got treated at the emergency room for his broken nose, he agreed to take the first swings in that fight. Aaron took him to an addiction and recovery center, where he enrolled. And stayed.

That act wasn't the same as slapping down the big joker, or even a trump card. It wasn't enough to build back up all the trust he'd betrayed. But it was a start.

I was proud of him. So was Ant.

Like I said at the beginning, the house always wins. But there's one other saying us Joplin men liked to throw around. *If you don't like your hand, try playing a different game.*

Ant was short. He was terrible at talking trash, he hated conflict, and he had a lot to learn about dealing with hard situations. But was he tough? Was he clever?

Shoot—is water wet?

So sure, there may not be any do-overs in the supreme game of life. No reshuffles or take-backs. And maybe you *do* have to play the cards you're dealt.

But if you're smart and brave—like my grandson Ant—you find a way to keep your cards and play a *new* game. One that suits the strengths of your hand.

And then you get to show the house—and the world—who's really unbeatable.

# RESOURCES FOR READERS

The characters in this book may be fictional, but substance abuse and addiction are all too real. However, just like Ant, you don't have to face these problems on your own. If you don't feel comfortable talking to a parent, teacher, friend, or other adult, you can always reach out to any of the organizations listed below. Trust me—there's nothing weak about asking for help.

**Alcoholics Anonymous (AA)** is an international support group for people who have a drinking problem. Anyone who wants to do something about their drinking problem can become a member. https://www.aa.org/

**Al-Anon** is a support group for the family and friends of people who abuse alcohol. Al-Anon members provide support and encouragement, whether the alcoholic seeks help or not. **Alateen** is a support group within Al-Anon that is specifically for teenagers who are impacted by alcoholics. https://al-anon.org

**Self-Management and Recovery Training (SMART Recovery)** is a community of support groups in which participants help one another resolve problems with any addiction (including alcohol dependence and gambling). **SMART Family & Friends** is a program that supports the friends and loved ones of those struggling with addiction. https://www.smartrecovery.org

**Substance Abuse and Mental Health Services Administration (SAMHSA)** has a 24-hours-a-day, 365-days-a-year phone service, in English and Spanish, for individuals facing substance abuse disorders or mental illness and their family members. This service provides information about local treatment facilities and support groups. 1-800-662-HELP (4357)

# ACKNOWLEDGMENTS

This book wouldn't exist without the help of so many people, starting with my agent, Sara Crowe, and my editor, Jenne Abramowitz, as well as Melissa Schirmer for production, Jessica White for copyediting, and Elizabeth Parisi for guiding the book cover and design process—with special appreciation going to Frank Morrison for bringing Ant to life with his amazing cover art! I would also like to thank the entire Scholastic family for their continued support, including Lizette Serrano, Emily Heddleson, Danielle Yadao, Matt Poulter, Elisabeth Ferrari, Erin Berger, and Ellie Berger.

Just like Ant is supported by the entire Oak Grove community, I wouldn't be the person I am today without the love and guidance of so many people from my youth. I cannot thank you all by name, but I am a better person because of everything each of you did.

Of all the spades players I've traded books and barbs with over the years, I want to give a special shout-out to

Job "Joe Mac" Milfort, who taught a scrawny sixteen-year-old a lot about spades, and even more about self-confidence.

To my VCFA and Beverly Shores friends, thank you for all the encouragement as you repeatedly listened to snippets of the novel, and always laughed at the funny parts.

And finally, to my family, thank you for your everlasting support. Sydney and Savannah, thank you for always believing that your dad can do anything if he tries hard enough. And Mom and Dad, thank you for being the best coaches that a kid could ask for in this great game of life.

# ABOUT THE AUTHOR

**VARIAN JOHNSON** is the author of several novels for children and young adults, including *The Parker Inheritance,* which won both Coretta Scott King Author Honor and *Boston Globe/Horn Book* Honor awards; *The Great Greene Heist,* an ALA Notable Children's book and *Kirkus Reviews* Best Book; and the graphic novel *Twins,* illustrated by Shannon Wright, an NPR Best Book. He lives with his family near Austin, Texas. You can visit him on the web at varianjohnson.com and @varianjohnson.